As If Something Happened

JULIE MURPHY

Relax. Read. Repeat.

AS IF SOMETHING HAPPENED
By Julie G. Murphy
Published by TouchPoint Press
Brookland, AR 72417
www.touchpointpress.com

Copyright © 2020 Julie Murphy
All rights reserved.

ISBN-13: 978-1-946920-92-8

Editor: Jenn Haskin
Cover Design: Colbie Myles
Cover image: Red Eye by Alessandro Grandini, Adobe Stock

Visit the author's website at juliegmurphy.wordpress.com

First Edition

Printed in the United States of America.

There are four people to whom I particularly want to dedicate this book. First off, Gabrielle Erken and Penelope Norton, L PHD. Gabby was with me through my brace days. To help me with an editing deadline, during her cruise on the Indian Ocean, she graciously did what English majors/editors do to books: picked mine apart and then pulled it back together. Also a big thank you to Penelope Norton, my friend and in-law relation who in her work in psychotherapy specializes in promoting healing and personal growth through understanding of self and others in children, teens, and adults. Always encouraging, she helped me shape the ending of the story.

I would also like to thank my two football experts, Coach Jim Hammond and Defensive Assistant Coach Matt Butterfield, for all their good advice and football play information—offensively and defensively.

Finally, I'd like to thank the Camp Morrison Boy Scout camp for the comprehensive tour of the camp and for showing me how to stack powder and ball into a muzzle-loader. I have to say it was quite gratifying to hit the target.

Chapter One

In Walmart, when I was five years old, I pleaded with my mom for a glittery, Cinderella dress. She kept walking down the aisle of store saying, "Oh darling, what do you want that for, you'd just play in it in the dirt and anyway you have the body of a square, defensive football player. I mean, you aren't tall, darling, and you have no waist. You poor thing, you've got your father's genes."

The only reason that I wanted that dress was because I was jealous in kindergarten of two girls who got to be the Indian princesses in the school play. My casting? Ragtime Joe who is, according to the song, 'high falutin', rootin'-tootin', a son of a gun from Arizona.' Don't get me wrong, it's a blast at five to be a rootin'-tootin' son-of-a-gun, but I saw early on that princesses have the good times rolling.

It took me a long time to learn that you may not grow tall, and your nose doesn't get any smaller because you really, really want it to; that long eyelashes are genetic, and mascara doesn't really make them longer.

It was my genes, my units of heredity, my characteristics that made my mother and the kindergarten teacher see me not as a pretty Indian lass, but with a six-shooter. Let me tell you, being Ragtime Joe has disadvantaged me. My mother and father combo, I call it gene cocktail.

Ok, I'm not a designer shoe or a home-run hitter or in any way suaaave and genteeeel. I get "B's" and "C's." I have short legs and square shoulders; and a booming voice. I say what I think and can't filter, because truth seems to be way too important to me.

Being so disadvantaged, at school I have been called Butt Monkey as in the butt of the joke, the girl in the red shirt, the stupid sidekick. I actually RESPOND to the monikers Elmur—thanks to Kirsten who in middle school used to shorten names—"L" for Laura and Murphy, my last name, equals "Elmur." So "Elmur Fudd." My stepdad once called me The Schnauzer. Laura, what my mother named me at birth, does not sound like the name of a defensive-end, stubborn-terrier kind of person. She hoped for better.

My mom divorced my defensive-line dad and remarried her tall, graceful prince and had two princess daughters and a prince junior. One dull day, I permanently dropped myself off at Gran's. I was too stocky for the new family, and I knew it. Good on Gran that she warmed to my arrival. She loves football and dogs.

That's why I can't wait. May fifth…Injection Day.

Stepping Away from "I"-ness.

That's what that day is OFFICIALLY called in hotspots all over the world. It will begin in the morning. Then every ninth grader, from randomly selected test schools, will be given a sort of "vaccination" of someone else's genes. Someone else's genetic code. What it's like to be someone else. Like being a real-life avatar.

Only we don't get to choose.

They tell us we might have a little tenderness in the injection area, and maybe a little dizziness, but like our childhood shots for measles and mumps, we'll all be fine.

Gran says, "Vaccinations my ass—more like allergy injections, sending something into the blood that can kill you; that you're allergic to. Mark my words, girl, there'll be trouble. Some people are anaphylactic towards each other."

I don't care. I want to know Stella Constance Miller's first, second and third thoughts every morning, and her last thought at bedtime. I want to be greeted when I walk into the gym. I want to stroll in the hallways as a group. I want to have social skills and have people to listen to me when I talk—like they do her. Either that or I want to be anyone who is a…graceful, saved-by-the-hero, pretty, *for crying out loud*, Indian princess.

"She isn't pretty at all," I say to my friend Andrew Holtus. "But that doesn't seem to matter. Why doesn't it matter? That's why I want her."

Across from me, in the living-room of the two-bedroom, green ranch house I share with Gran, I cannot actually see Andrew roll his eyes behind his reality goggles, but I know. We've been friends since pre-school, I always played with the boys, and he liked to be with the girls. Anyway, he's tired of my princess hang-up. Once he asked me why I wanted to be someone else.

Friends. People who actually call and ask if I can come over.

"She has good hair. Guys like her long, black, straight hair. I saw her giving Sam Smith a quickie shoulder massage yesterday before the algebra teacher came into the classroom. A shoulder massage, pfffttt."

I miss a demon kill and Andrew is run though. He punches my upper arm. Both of us whip off our goggles.

"The shot isn't going to give you long black hair."

"It will make me think that my short, mousey hair is superior. I won't be calling it short, mousey hair."

He collapses onto Gran's tribal, red, green, and beige, itchy sofa and throws popcorn into his mouth while we wait for a reset.

I drop next to him and grab a handful and spill kernels onto the dark brown carpet. We both throw our feet onto the coffee table. Its surface has enough water rings to be a design. No figurines, or vases, or coasters (obviously) or boxes with hidden treasures.

"If I don't have them, I don't have to dust them. If the carpet looks like dirt it won't show the dirt," Gran says.

Andrew likes to come to my house because it's comfortable here and laid-back. Like Gran's skin, everything is dull from age and faded from sun, and with brown spots, so no fuss. That is, except for her leather recliner in front of the TV (to put her feet up), and my shiny, black gaming system. When I moved in with Gran, she bought it for me. I don't know if it was a pity gift, or just something that would keep me busy.

"Can you just play?" Andrew begs in a fed-up-with-my-chatter tone.

"How can I? We are becoming someone else…in real time. I mean, how can you not think about it?"

Andrew doesn't respond. He has already eaten to the popcorn duds at the bottom of the bowl. Andrew is sort of long and starved looking, all legs and ears, from his tofu diet. He is always hungry. His eyes are large and kind of liquidly. I come up to his knobby knees. I'm a mix terrier to his large breed dog. He's already so tall that at my height, five feet, three inches, I have to bend back my neck to look at his face in the clouds. Sometimes I make him stand just right so he blocks the sun, and it isn't burning out my eyeballs.

"I don't want to be anybody different from me or anybody at all," he says with his hand in front of his full mouth. He hates people who talk with their mouth full of masticated mush.

"They should've let us pick. I want her because she knows stuff, like trendsetting, how-to with guys. She's a fashionista. She has a web site with followers, lots of them. What do you think it would be like, me as Stupendous Stella and then in three weeks going back to who I am? Will I be distraught?"

"Definitely. Come on let's just play."

4

"Who will have to be me?" I ask as I put on my goggles again. Andrew doesn't bite and lets the question hang as he follows me into the game. I swing my virtual sword and cut off the head of a goblin as it charges me from the castle hall. The goblin gone, I ask Andrew, "What happens if you get someone really weird?"

The trolls are upon us now. I move back to back with Andrew.

"I suppose too that if I get Stupendous Stella, I would be mocking myself. *Shenanigans*. It's a whole new level of self-torment. I mean that COULD happen."

As I hear myself saying the words. I feel stabbed through the heart. As if in stereo, a goblin sneaks up and slices me too. I'm virtually dead, again.

"If you aren't going to pay attention, I'm not playing anymore."

I strip off my goggles. I glance at my reflection in the front of them. I study my eagle eyes; zits that won't go away no matter what products I use; a nose that is too big for my miniature face; a mouth that is too small for my liberal nose. "I really hate my small mouth. Gran says it's her mouth, and that I should have picked my Aunt Lucy's. I make kissy lips.

Andrew rests his goggles above his gray eyes that have the long lashes I crave. "Would you just stop talking about it? I don't want to think about it. Let's just play so we can level up."

I stick out my tongue at him and then pout. "How can we not? I mean it's like so huge. It's the-I-kid-you-not elephant in the room."

"So you want to be the person that makes your life miserable."

"She doesn't make everyone's life miserable. People like her. Anyway, I don't want to BE her. I just want to know HOW to be her. As they said, a whole new perspective."

"Look, I like you and all your weird just fine, and this all is stupid, and I don't want to do any of it."

It's true. Call me skeptoid, about the principal saying now that we've had five-sixths of a year of high school, have become older, more mature from our pre-teen and early-teen behaviors, that this is a chance to integrate more fully, to be closer friends to each other, and kinder, see each other more clearly. *Ha! Let's see him do it.*

The swapped genetic material decays over the three weeks and becomes waste. My genetic material could become waste in Stupendous Stella. God, that's too much to think about. On the other hand, her genetic codes could become waste in me. Superb.

"What if I get brace-girl Alice Ochoa? They said that if the person you get has a wheelchair or something, you'll have to use it. I'd have to come to school in that thingy she wears. I couldn't bend at the waist or look down. I'd have to come to school in a tent. Absodefinitely, I don't know how she gets in and out of a car. She can hardly pick up a book from the ground. She walks around like she's a shadow. No sir, thanks much."

"Be kind. It's not Alice's fault."

"I know. I know. Arrrgghhh. I just don't want to be worse off; you know? Just for the three weeks, I want to know what's it's like to be socially advanced."

"Alice's ok."

"Alice. I know, but she needs more something. To be a successful brace girl, she needs more A-type genes. She needs to be a Connor Mackenzie. A joke for every reason, you know less…sensitive. She needs to use her personality to make her brace invisible to people. If genetics gives you lemons, it should also have to give you the personality to make lemonade."

Genetic engineering couldn't fix poor old Alice's problem, a missing growth center on her spine because her mother drank or something. It also doesn't fix personality traits like hate, greed, shyness. It's too hard to fix flat feet, or oily skin, or pimples. To those who say it's character building, I say booyah.

A horn outside honks three times, and then a pause, and then again.

"It's your mom."

Andrew and I eyeball each other. Fear freezes us both.

"How are we going to get through this tomorrow?" he blurts out. Andrew is not a blurter.

A sudden anxiety spike is making me feel like throwing up. Andrew has gone chalky.

"We have a pinky swear?" he asks.

"Of course we pinky sweared. I will be there for you, and you will be there for me no matter who be become. We are best friends. Always. No mind melt will blow that out."

Andrew picks up his coat and opens the door. "I don't think I can do this."

"Yes you can, you will. Besides, with me as another person you might get to the next level." I try to smile, but Andrew's face is just breaking my heart.

I close the door. I inhale the scent of Gran's living room, the bite of it from old, stuffed furniture, infrequently vacuumed carpets, winter snow-damp and spring mud, with cinnamon on top from all the rice puddings she bakes.

In my bedroom, I cocoon into my old, yellow blankie, with Zee Zee the zebra cuddled against my neck. We are becoming someone else. We don't get to pick who we are, and we can't take them off by raising our goggles. I think about tomorrow and wonder if I should be more choosy than usual about what to wear.

Chapter Two

Today, injection day, is colder. The air smells of melting snow and mud. May is the worst month for weather. There is a herd of deer that wanders through the pines between the houses. I see them as I walk to school. They stand in the middle of the street and stare. They don't move, not even for cars. Gran has a deer feeder in her yard, so they won't eat her daisies. They still do.

I listen to the constant drip of melting snow in stereo as Andrew lumbers along behind me. We are dressed the same in different sizes, hoodies, and jeans, extra-long and petite. I walk in zigzag, trying to miss the deeper puddles in the winter-broken asphalt. I use spongy grass or beds of pine needles to keep my shoes dry. The sky is weirdly not rainy-gray, but bright blue and happy with pure white clouds. Birds are singing.

When I was younger and stressed-out, and I'd see a rainbow, I'd say to myself that the world is showing me that everything will be alright, and when it wasn't, I quit depending on weather for predictions of my future.

The school is new, all glass and metal. It has parking in front and game fields the rest of the way around it. The baseball field is covered to keep it dry. There is a skateboard park along a far road and a mountain-biking park.

My wet sneakers squeak on the floor of Chief Joseph High School. There are teachers at the door. "Freshmen go straight to the gym," they are saying over and over like machines. I'm having a hard time keeping breakfast down. Andrew hasn't said a word the whole walk.

Ahead of me I see Shaun, the Sheep, Murphy, no relation, stop short of crossing the threshold. He turns and heads for the street. With heart-thumping hope, he picks up speed. Nope. They've got teachers stationed outside as well.

Seriously. Where is a good enveloping fog when you need it?

With a three-fourths of Chief Joseph High student body excused, the clanging sound of the metal bleachers sounds like it's muffled. We still gather by habit in the freshmen section. The expanse of empty seats makes me shiver. We are pretty much alone in this.

The high school freshman class has ninety-nine students. With that number, they could have let Shaun go free, but then he wouldn't be the only one to try to bolt.

They say the school was picked by lottery. I say it was picked because we are a tiny lake town, miles from civilization, without much technical access, and expendable. Also short on cash, so bribable.

I can feel my seat bounce from the weight and movement of a hundred bodies. It's a colorful group, red sweaters, yellow shirts, blue pants, and some individuals in tie-dye, others in black. The colors are a rainbow effect, but like I said, no prediction of success, though the teachers and administration, who are standing at the door or behind a rolled-in podium, are smiling their rainbow smiles so hard that their faces may break. Their forced, faked optimism is ignored. They are making us pop out, and are collecting the nano-phones in our eyes, our ear-pods and phones. Whatever anyone has. The biggest sin? They are taking away our music. I can live without texting, but not music. People are yell-complaining. Why, they are asking. Ridiculous. Are they afraid someone will call the police for help?

I watch the class. While some glare at any supervisor in eye shot, others call out to one another. They are moving in ordered lines, and I hear someone say, "Baaaa." It gets few laughs.

Stella steps in surrounded, as she always is, by people with perfect noses and skin, startling eye color and hair, or some other boost of natural selection. I study her again. No, she is not even close to pretty, but a real confidence lights her eyes, and she has a way with people. She makes them feel important. I itch to be her. I dream about what it would be like to be anticipated.

The heavy, velvet curtains in front of the stage along the far side of the gym are closed, like they are hiding something. The official podium has been rolled out onto the shiny wooden floor. The basketball hoops are retracted back. We are not here to play ball; or are we?

The principle is at the microphone calling for us to be seated. He is short and square with pants that are loose against his thin thighs. The podium hides all but his chest, which is adorned in a professionally pressed blue shirt and in an "I-ness" Day tie. His head is a perfect circle with ears. We call him C.B., Charlie Brown, or Van Lichtenstein. He carries a WWII German baton that he taps on your shoulder when he wants your attention.

He generally reeks of cigarette smoke which he tries to cover up with cheap cologne and mint lozenges. He tries to be a kind guy who, as he says, carries a big stick. *Carrot and ssstick*, he says a lot. It's supposed to be funny…carrot and ssstick. His voice is deep, and it sounds like it should be coming from a larger man. He's not wishy-washy. He can command an audience. Today, he's CB the car salesman. I sense his nerves are stretched. His face is pale and pinched. He'll really be working his audience, carrot and ssstick.

To get us to sit down, the teachers are making down motions with arms extended and their palms facing the floor. They are still smiling. After some minutes, there is an awful silence. Later, someone coughs, and another giggles. The majority of the class have their heads down, their hands clasped. Some couples lean into each other. The principal's monotone is a bulkhead holding back an agitated and rising sea. As he speaks, his gaze pinpoints faces in the crowd, faces he knows to be uncooperative. Yes, this is for you, Tom Smith, and you, Marissa Delgado, and Zak Lancaster, and you Shaun.

"Quiet everyone. Quiet, quiet. Thank you. This is a big day. You are all going to experience for the first time ever in the world something that will change society as we know it." He calls instructions into the air, to the computer assistant "Alexia." A three-D talking head of the President of the United States appears, and floats above the principal's head. Must be Kaiser's first sell-out, tech purchase. May God have mercy on his soul.

It speaks. "As you all know, genetic engineering has provided a great service to mankind."

Mankind?! We're fifteen-year-olds.

"The world is experiencing chronic conflict, small constant wars around the globe that are unending. People die, children die, and entire generations of the young, people your ages, are mentally scarred for life. Today is The Day that we try to bring people together as they have never been brought together before. You all should feel privileged to be the first in the world to bring peace for all time. This social exchange—"

This social experiment, Mr. President. Call a "spade" a "spade."

"—is taking place in schools all over the world, and in one school in each of the fifty states. That of itself is quite an achievement. Many of you may already be benefactors of genetic engineering. In your lifetime diseases like cystic fibrosis, severe combined immunodeficiency, even the common cold, have been engineered out of our lives. As scientists work with genotype, they are finding ways to change metabolism and memory. Someday students will never have to take spelling tests ever again."

The principal pauses the President to let the teachers laugh and clap. Yay. Back to the President.

"Every one of us now has a password to our personal DNA on file at the National Health Service. In your files are your gene sequences, gene variants and combinations that show your vulnerabilities. We have extracted your DNA and synthesized your personal variants. You have all filled out, along with your parents, a questionnaire on your personal development, family history, and specific personality symptoms."

I didn't listen after that. I'm thinking of Carly. At age five and a half, they tried to increase her metabolism, but she is still fat. I remember overhearing her resigned voice mumbling during third period biology. I forget what the exact subject was, but she was saying, "All life is an autonomous agent that is working on its own behalf. Sometimes when the human body is put into non-equilibrium, it strives for equilibrium." It boils down to her body likes things the way they are. To be in Zen with itself, her body needs to be fat.

I glance over at Stupendous Stella again. She is whispering to her group. She is pointing out people and laughing. I think of genetic variables, and I think that she's always had one missing—kindness, but that is not what I'm looking for. Nobody makes it on kindness.

I pick up on a line the President is saying, "Your school officials have already designated match-ups by personality differentials. Your matchups will expand your points of view. You will no longer be confined by your own thoughts and reactions. You will experience the world in a whole different way. You will be wearing, for a brief time, another person's shoes."

This catches everyone's attention. There is shuffling and general whispering in the ranks. The buzz fills the large room as if a switch has been flipped and has created electrical static, a quiet hum.

The principal is watching us like a vulture on a perch, shoulders hunched: his eyes penetrating as he scans the crowd for prey, that one student dying to be out of order.

The image of the president recedes. It's back to Lichtenstein. We are all listening now. "As I said, after the vaccination, you won't know whose genetic point of view you will be sharing. That's not important. This will be done in alphabetical order. No one will know who they are, just that they are experiencing someone other than themselves for the next three weeks. Scientists have been removing genetic material from one organism and transferring it to another for years now, even between species. Trials on human volunteers have been successful. This is perfectly safe."

Mumbling from the herd.

"Quiet, quiet. You are to keep a daily journal for the next three weeks. You will be graded on the journal. Also, you will write a paper about your experience. Depending on what we see in the papers, we may reveal at the end who you were. We haven't decided yet."

Now…we've already extensively answered all your questions on this. After you get your variations-gene-carrying retrovirus, go straight to your home room."

I am "M" for Murphy. Once the "A"s have gone, the air comes to life again. An ancient movie begins.

For an hour people leave and never come back. It is like they've been taken to gas chambers. The boys get the gym teacher to bring out basketballs, but the hoops stay fixed in place. The girls cluster and talk. Andrew is an "H"—Holtus. He has left me. He is becoming someone I might not like. My heart feels like it's in the spin-cycle of the washer. I'd stared at him the whole way to the door, until he walked through it and disappeared. This is becoming too real. I don't want to play anymore.

"M!" an enhanced voice calls.

The M's march as condemned young men and women to the auditorium where we see tables. The first of the sets of tables have signs that say: Ma-Me, Mf-Mj, Mk-Mo. My ears buzz. I blink my eyes because the letters swim. The room is hot, I take off my navy sweatshirt, when I do it trembles in my hands. I move forward. Am I breathing? I have to be breathing. Mp-Mz.

"Murphy," I say. "Laura."

"Your hands are ice," the adult volunteer says to me as she hands me a pen to sign off on my name.

I move the two glaciers that my feet have become to get in line for my shot. Twenty are ahead of me. I need to scream so much that I fear I will. Stella is in the line next to mine. She will go before me. Over the ringing in my ears, I can hear the voices of the volunteer parents, "Over here please," or of the nurses, "Next." I feel like I'm going to throw up on the pants of the girl in front of me. Teresa McPhee will have my chunks on her one-size-too-small, designer-jeans. She will scream at me and call me an idiot. Would that stop things?

I can see from the shell-shocked glint in everyone's eyes that we are all going to throw up. It's like explosive diarrhea bad. We are shuffling in our lines like institutionalized drug addicts.

And then, someone finally flips. Stella. It is like she's been shot chock-full of poison. Be it from pain of the shot, or from the needle in her arm, or from watching the liquid of someone else's genes being plunged into her arm, first she quivers, and then fits. She lets out a demon scream, and then it's like the devil takes her soul. Profanity pours from her lips. She hauls back and slaps the first adult to grab her arm. It sounds through the room with perfect projection. She kicks at the next adult that tries to subdue her and spits in his face. Total nuclear meltdown. She throws herself at an exit door. Her straight, black hair is a hard frame for her washed-out face. She sprints out the door like the variants given to her are adrenaline charged. She is gone. Her system absodefinitely can't absorb being someone else. An alarm blares into every corner of the school. It's an emergency-only exit. It sure is.

The room erupts in voices and sounds like an aviary of nervous parrots. A few parents follow her, but after twenty minutes they return. She only had about one hundred yards to a patch of forest of aspen and pine and low growing huckleberry bushes. All the adults are now in panic and yelling at each other.

The nurses are still holding needles. They suddenly seem like a coven of mad scientists who are in possession of death syringes. If this were a game, I would now, as they are distracted, impale them on my sword, one after the other...like the dervish Stupendous Stella had become.

The students are watching the adults with a fixed attention the teachers wish they had in the classroom. The alarm shuts down. I feel the quiet in my bones. "Stop the injections," booms over the speaker system. "All freshmen students to home room."

And then I hear, they all hear, "Laura Murphy...come to the office immediately."

As the principal said, none of us know the personality matchups, but it seems pretty obvious to me that Stella got a dose of me shot into her bloodstream, and I caused her to go insane. Even though that's not what I wanted, but what I dreaded, in fact, my worst nightmare...I do have to smile. Bingo.

Chapter Three

Stella Constance Miller got me. I've never been surer of anything in my life as I'm being marched out of the auditorium and down the hall to the first door on the left and then into the main office. I hear more than see the frothing of trouble deep inside the core of the building. I'm led behind the counter to a nearby door.

My first words, as I fall into the generic seat on the other side of Principal Kaiser's big brown desk are, "She doesn't know does she?"

"Of course she wasn't told. We just don't know," he snaps like a triggered bear trap. "We don't know what's happening. The police have responded."

The secretary pokes her hairspray scented head in the door. "They want to know should they clear out the room."

"Yes. Have the hospital secure the serum."

"What about the others, the injected ones? Should their parents come get them earlier?"

"Oh my Lord." Kaiser swivels his chair towards the window. I see him close his eyes. I realize how delicate it has all been. Andrew is not Andrew anymore, and I am me, and another me is running around loose in the city like a dangerous zoo animal that has freed itself by gnawing off its arm, and it doesn't know anything but the walls around its own cage. She's never, ever considered the world from any other perspective but her own.

Right now, I'm glad I'm me, and I'm sad I'm me. I'm unhappy that I have to watch Andrew be someone else. I want to strike the man behind the desk. My hands ball into fists.

The Principal stands and walks to the door. The secretary shuts the door behind both of them. After a few minutes in the office alone with the scent of his cologne and residual smoke, I open a mint from the candy jar and toss it into my mouth and suck on it. I haven't asked, but I feel I'm due. I'm immediately sorry as the smell of mint mixes with the other odors and makes me more nauseous.

I stand at his window beside the floor lamp and the two, high backed, floral armchairs he uses for friendly conversations when the carrot and ssstick don't work. The day is sunny and beautiful. The grass is greening, a willow is budding. Squirrels are playful in the new warmth.

I feel like taking the red highlighter from his pencil holder and writing "stupid" in huge letters across the top sheet of some papers on his desk. I glance at the wording already there. The injection list. I freeze. He'd been reading it, of course, to find my name. The urge to be someone else hits me like a tsunami. I glance at the door. Me looking up who I would have been would be a small problem to his day. Tempting me further, the "M's" are on top. I don't need to touch anything to see my name. My ears prick for a click of the doorknob. I scan the list to my name. Next to Laura Murphy is Enid O'Brien.

Noooo are you joking! The whole I-kid-you-not package!

Thrill tingles in my heart and through my spine. The Holy Grail of freshmen. Someone I wouldn't have the nerve to dream about being. I realize that I am missing out big time, again. I am the victim here. I curse the school, the principal, the universe. I have the absodefinitely worst luck. Pfffttt.

When Kaiser returns half an hour later, he has an army of adults behind him who are not smiling like they were this morning.

"We can't locate Stella," Kaiser says to me as he sits and swivels towards me.

"Where would you go? What would you do?" he asks leaning in. They are all staring at me. I am staring back with the must truculent, mean-eyed look I can place on my face, and it's not hard. I don't want to help them. It's their problem. What I want is to take Enid O'Brien's personality out for a spin.

"Look, I say scooting forward in my chair. "Stella will turn up. Believe me. I'm not an outgoing type. I don't like streets at night. I don't like the dark. I will get hungry."

I'm lying because I can. What I'd really do is go home to my room and lose myself in my games. As I think the words, I would go to my room, I inhale sharply. The exhale sounds like extreme swearing. She couldn't. She doesn't know who she is blending with, does she?

They, those in charge of this explosive diarrhea of a thing, press in closer to me. Their collective breath is hot. The pressure of a lost student makes their faces shine with sweat.

I explode like Stella did. It's like I have fireworks in my head, shimmering lights. The bang, bang, is the sound of my anger. My vision is smoky and explosions fill my inner ear. These stupid people. They don't get anything.

Principal Kaiser stares at me. He is trying to contain the situation, and here he has another student off the rails.

"What about Andrew Holtus? How is he?" I spit out at him in a snide voice.

"He's in homeroom. He's fine. It's Stella that isn't fine."

"Yeah right. You people. She's not me. She would never blend with me. Don't ask me where she would go, because I HAVE NO IDEA."

"She is becoming like you." Mr. Kaiser hammers each word. "Laura, you have to find yourself. How hard can that be?"

Find myself! "Impossible," I yell at him. I want to laugh like a hysterical hyena. Find myself! Oh yes, how hard can THAT possibly be!

IDIOT.

All I wanted from this disaster was to find out about someone else, like Enid. I can't be a princess. I can't be Enid. Anger makes a fist-ball in my gut. Emotions make me want to yell at his how-hard-can-that-be face; or cry as if I'm at my own funeral. I want to swing at him like Stella did, but I can't. She can, I can't.

"Look, I'll bring Andrew here."

"Which one? Where actually is he?" I ask like Andrew is a real concern of his; like he really knows. I squeeze my eyelids together so that I can stop any moisture gathering there. Andrew and me, need to get lost in some primordial forest in a place no one can guess, so we can get through all this with a quiver of dignity. Pfffttt the rest of all this. I do what every student through time does when they need to escape; I tell them what they want to hear, locations, whatever. Whatever gets them off my back.

Some luck for me then. The secretary again distracts Kaiser. A student is vomiting all over the biology classroom, which happens in biology most of the time anyway.

His face reads like a whole string of fully ripe swear words. All the adults follow him. One with the group, I squeeze out the gap.

In the hallways, weeks before The Day, I heard plenty of opinions about what was to go down. If she had to be someone, brainy Allyson would be Krista. She wanted to know what it was like to be stacked, dyed, and foolish, same with skinny Brad, for boys. He wanted to be locked and loaded. It became a game. Most of the people in the class were reduced to superlatives by their peers, or to a joke to help keep people brave. The middle "M's" through "Z's" got lucky, the not-injected group. Not Andrew, who never speculated; mild Andrew, who just wanted to be left alone.

He is alone right now. Promise broken. Where is he? Desperation pounds on the pain in my head. I have to find him.

It's easy to get lost into hallways full of disjointed teenagers, and it's hard to move though them. Kaiser doesn't know where Andrew Holtus is. Not homeroom, that's for sure. Andrew is predictable. I find him just where I know he will be, in the empty chemistry room in the back corner by the racks. He must have gone there as a way to preserve himself while he was still himself. He was transforming. He'd gone through that all alone. He didn't want to do this but has; I did but then didn't. My heart feels bloodshot. I just want to take his hand and lead him out of here.

He is under a table, his knees to his chest, his head down. Andrew loves this classroom with its stained tabletops and odor of sulfur. He likes the smell of chemicals. The wall paint is not white anymore. The room is bright with the light of the day. Some glass bottles channel the light into a prism of colors, another stupid rainbow. Others are badly cleaned, dull, and opaque. Now there's a metaphor for life. There is no one else in the classroom. People have had enough of foul chemistry already.

I hesitate. Who is he? I forgot to look. How could I forget to check that? Normally, I'd sneak up behind him, and then he would say something like, "You stalking' me?" all gangster-like because he likes antique movies. I can't do it with him all tight-in on himself.

I call Shitnanigans.

I get really close, and say in a real soft voice, "Hey Andrew, are you ok?"

After what seems an extended super-senior moment, he turns his narrowed eyes to my face and just says, "What, hey."

That could be Andrew. It could be anybody. Idiot tears, I backhand them. I have to wait for a moment so I can talk. It feels like my heart-muscle has fused. "For the love of God, Andrew, how are you?"

He doesn't answer.

"Andrew!"

Nothing.

This is not good. Shifting to sit next to him, I inhale to the bottom of my lungs the acidic smells of the room. He would want me to get him out. I don't know how to get him out.

As if trying to make a clearance, Andrew is shaking his head and blinking his eyes. I wonder if someone got him. Maybe his genes weren't used in somebody else. There are two of me, and at this point possibly none of him, because he just doesn't seem to be here. I'm waiting and thinking and ready to pound anyone who comes near him. I'm thinking ambulance and remember our phones are gone, and then his eyes sort of clear, like the message triangle in a fortune telling ball. When he says to me, "Well if it isn't 'Elmur's' glue," I fall back on my butt as if I'd been hit.

This isn't supposed to happen. They said we'd be ourselves. They lied. They are lying, liars of the worst kind; people in charge whom we are meant to believe. "Why is this happening? Why is he someone else?" I scream a question at Eloise the voice activated computer.

Eloise's answer stuns me to my core: "Intertwined in biology, especially human biology, is self-awareness. The cells, combine to this ultimate goal to some degree in all living creatures." Figures. The injected genes are working towards their goal. They don't know they've been transplanted. They've found a nice warm brain in a nice warm skull with a blood supply. What else didn't they tell us? My friend is gone or in some corner of his brain hiding until this is over. That sounds like Andrew.

Peter Farber, only insane gods with a grudge would have thought all this up. It must have been very hilarious in that dark hole they were in when they said to each other—*how about we pair tall, skinny, mild mannered Andrew with, Peter the Pumpkin-Eater, the kid who ran screaming in a*

*pharmacological rage at a car, and who is now in a
wheelchair while he grows new legs. The kid who likes to eat
tripping seeds.*

No wonder Andrew was glassy-eyed. Pfffttt…the world
has gone absodefinitely ridiculous.

I stare at the shell of my best friend, and try to locate
where, in his skull, Andrew is lurking, I hope is lurking. He
looks well enough; his color is coming back. I pray the two
personalities don't ignite. Hopefully, Andrew loves
chemistry and Peter likes chemicals in his own way. I said
I'd keep him safe until this is over, and I will.

May Kaiser rot for bringing this down upon us for new
computers. He is, they are, the dung-heap of life. I think of
Stella. I wonder if she is sitting zombie-like under some table
or running around barking and snapping like a rabid dog that
needs to be put down. I wonder if my genes are acting like
some brain-eating virus in her head. That's a turnaround. I
have a painful stab of sympathy for her.

"Andrew." Maybe I can draw him out. "You remember
that we all were given injections," I say with enunciation. I
have no idea what a "converted model" would or would not
know. "Andrew are you in there at all?" There is a
quickening to his face and interest in his eyes. "Andrew, you
have become Peter Farber. Can you hear me? YOU ARE
PUMPKIN-EATER." God, I may have just seen him
grimace. Andrew will be back. They wouldn't do this if
things didn't get back to normal in the end, would they? I
just don't know anymore. "Stella went looney-toons when
she was injected with me. Ipso Fatso refused."

"Heavy inconvertible evidence?"

I double take Andrew. "Hey wait…oh, ha." I drop my
head and press my lips together to control the anger pressing
against my skin. It IS Peter. Peter's mission in life is to make
fun of my malapropisms.

"Frankly my dear," I drawl.

He laughs. "Stella got you?" Andrew's lips say in

22

Peter's defined drawl that he affects to let the world know that he's absodefinitely, unapologetically laid back.

Shocked at the chemically-induced schizophrenic that my friend has become, I stare at his face that has lost its sweet softness and has taken on a cynical glare. As I study the Peter/Andrew combination, I remember the word Chimera from biology class, and then Mrs. Montgomery saying, "Human Chimeras actually exist when one person has the genetic makeup of two separate individuals, as in the case of twins, the two embryos merge leaving only one fetus. There is a woman who in her cheeks has the genes of one embryo and in her ovary cells, the genes of the other.

Peter and Andrew are not twins. Their combination is more like half-human, half-donkey-breath. Left to his own, Peter would put Andrew's body through a drug and alcohol binge. My heart breaks for my tofu-eating friend. This is exactly what he didn't want…to give his body to science. He didn't want to look stupid, or to have stories told about him after this is over.

I hear my name over the loudspeaker. I throw a beaker at it. The sound of glass shattering is less than satisfying, considering. I know that I have to get Andrew out and home.

"Laura Murphy to the office," crackles the intercom. Now, I'm glad I'm not Enid. Pfffttt Enid. I have to get Andrew out of here. I think about how I am going to do that with everyone looking for me.

Chapter Four

Just last week in home economics, the teacher brought up babysitting and gave us a scenario such as what if there is a fire. I blurted out that I don't get paid enough to do fires. Sword-in-my-side Stella across from me, said, "God, what a despicable thing to say." She could have cut out my tongue. The effect would have been the same. Inside I bled all over. The shift of blood from my head to my heart made my brain numb. I couldn't feel the pencil in my hand. I couldn't say that it was just a joke with my tongue gone. Anyway, I could see in hindsight that it wasn't funny.

Even without Andrew, I wouldn't go looking for her because I don't want her to be found. Good riddance. Only she really hadn't…disappeared. If only.

Peter-Andrew is still hazy. I walk to the classroom door and look out the narrow strip of window. Everyone is everywhere. The original versions huddle together as a security precaution while some of the injected can't quite remember their names, the blend is too vague, whether they ride the bus, or their locker combinations. They should all be in home room. Can't lock them in if they do get there. Some of "The Injected" run out of bathrooms in tears or screaming.

Mirrors. The blend is too one-sided. I don't know who Mandy the goth-girl, got, but the blend inside her is doing both, screaming and crying.

I asked my Gran once why she didn't take sleeping pills for her insomnia. She has an awful time sleeping. She told me that some brains don't like to give over control. For her, the more the sleeping drug tried to put her to sleep, the more her brain tried to keep her awake.

"Remember that surgery I had," she said. "I was just out of the anesthetic at about midnight. I couldn't sleep, they gave me one then grudgingly two sleeping pills, and I was awake all night. Enough to drive anybody crazy needing to sleep but can't. Some people are asleep and awake at the same time. I swore off 'em. Nasty things. Better to leave the brain alone."

The "I-ness" experiment is bust. This is what happens when we are forced to share, share, and share ourselves. Kindergarten on steroids. The administration, the government, our parents had talked so much about it, and now it's pandemonius. Teacher are barking orders at the barking mad. The volunteer parents, the ones so supportive of the idea, are in teens' faces asking who they are. I could laugh.

Those in charge refer to lists, pages and pages of lists. With pinched faces, they say, "Let's see, you're paired with Bonnie…or Harry…or Sam…Jean." They're trying to sound soothing, only really, the hallway smells stressful. Stress BO. The school told mothers and fathers to pick up their children today. The parents will be arriving in two hours.

With this experiment, we were told, we all would become more accepting of each other; there would be less bullying, less putdowns, less hate. Gazing out at the human traffic pounding the plastic tiles in front of me, I'd say that we have never looked worse. Guinea pigs. I mean, don't most of us try and hide our demons and desires? I couldn't see the possibility of a harmonious Andrew and Peter at the end of this. In four weeks, they did promise change. Indeed, we won't be able to look each other in the face.

"Laura Murphy to the office," crackled the loudspeaker.

Time to go home. Andrew's body is beginning to curve and slump like Peter's signature position. A panic button slams down in some thinking part of my brain. They told us that we would remain ourselves with an enhancement. That's what they said. We would feel, "another's point of view." Andrew's expression has turned from lopsided, cautious interest, to the knitted brows of a cynical teen. God help him.

"Eloise," I say into the air. "Wouldn't virtual reality have been better than genetic swapping?" It glows, and pictures of philosophers pop up like measles on the white background. A disembodied voice begins an analysis. "The only source of Knowledge is experience, Albert Einstein."

"Why not virtual reality."

"Virtual reality tests the limits of stage reality not physical reality."

"Miss Laura Murphy TO THE OFFICE."

"They want you," he speaks. Peter-Andrew is coming to life. Come to think of it, Andrew would like that statement, "coming to life."

"Life's circumstances are requesting for me to go and find myself," I say over my shoulder to him.

Peter laughs, like I'm a comedian giving a punch line.

"It's not funny."

"'Bout time, Elmur." The ghost of a drawl is getting stronger.

"I don't know what you mean, donkey-breath. Anyway, it's like you, the kettle, calling the pot black." Andrew's body is becoming an avatar for Peter, and I'm talking to it. So the game has begun. I've always had Andrew's back. I won't let Peter run him into the ground.

"Find yourself?" He pauses and then snaps his fingers. I

know then that the transformation is complete, Andrew hates people who snap their fingers, like calling waiters—snap to my command. "More like, good God, Elmur has done another runner."

"Slick, Sherlock. Why does Stella hate me anyway? What reason have I ever given her to hate me? I don't talk to her. I don't engage her. She's just this bloodhound sniffing out all my mistakes."

"Did you know that if a monkey pulls a lever to get food, and when he pulls it another monkey gets shocked, even though he's starving he won't pull the lever again especially if he'd been in the hot seat before. Fast forward to the same experiment only with humans. Not only do the humans pull the lever they do it over and over and over."

"Bite me. Both of you."

He shrugs.

"Even if I find Sterling Stella, what do I do with her, take her home with me? We put on the virtual goggles, unwrap a bar of chocolate turn on the tea kettle and kick back?"

"Well she got you...gets you now."

"Maybe she'll grow to like me." We both burst laughing.

"Laura Murphy, come to the office immediately."

"It's your worst nightmare, Elmur."

I think I hear a touch less sarcasm, or do I just want to believe that Andrew is coming forth.

I hear my name again only closer, at the classroom door. The handy-dandy, snooping robot, the second acquired tech the school got for taking place in this dream experiment, has been sent out to search for me. I grab Peter and pull his arm to get him to run with me. My fear and momentum drag his butt across the floor some, but mostly my shoulder yanks back.

"Come on. Get up!" I yell.

He is using his arms to right himself. "How stupid are you anyway?" he yells at me. "What are you doing? God, my legs."

"Peter, idiot, it's Andrew's body. YOU CAN WALK."

"Elmur, idiot, no I can't."

"You are so messed up." I say between ground teeth.

From the open classroom door, I can hear the principal's voice booming at people to get to their classrooms. He's close. I hear the words "lock down." He is becoming desperate.

"For crying out loud, seriously!" One last glance at Andrew, two words: "Stay there." And I'm gone, out the classroom's second door and into the hallway that is still thick with people, all with Peter's laughter in my ears.

"Run, girl, run," he yells. At least I know he isn't going anywhere fast, or anytime soon.

As I bounce off students, I wonder what Stella will pay with her own body to get whatever she is planning against me. The girl has access to all my hopes and fears, my love interests, and failures. Oh God, please no. I do hate her for making me always feel so ashamed.

I dart around the labyrinth of hallways trying to think of where to get a wheelchair. I figure that the original Peter is still using his. No matter if his new personality thinks it can walk, Peter's body's leg function is limited. Get Andrew to a safe place. That is my priority. Stella will not go underground, but I will. That's the way it's always been. If I'm not around to watch her make a fool of me, then it won't bother me so much.

I bang into Mrs. Norton.

"Dear, Principal Kaiser has been calling you."

"I know, I'm just going there now."

"Hurry, dear."

I'm glad that Mrs. K is too well-thinking to even guess that I am not on my way to the office. I step around Jenny who is on the floor, her back against the wall, her knees up to her chest. She is sobbing.

"It's ok, I'm sure you got someone decent," Susan is saying to her. Across the hall a boy is flexing his muscles for the world or at least for the pool of people around him. A wimp gets the bod, even if he really doesn't, and it's all in his head. I feel happy for him. Isn't all of it, *just in our heads?*

My name is on the loudspeaker again. The voice is sounding much sterner. They must have more than the bot on my trail by now.

The only place I can think of to get a wheelchair is the nurse's office, which is connected to the main office. I have to go there. Maybe they won't be looking for me so close to ground zero.

I creep up on the front of the school. There is a line out the door and down the hallway of the nurse's office. The fire alarm is next to me. *It would serve them right.* I glance around me. *Someone would get hurt.* Students are mobbing the nurse's office, if I keep my head down, I'll just be one more student in the crowd. I have always been someone who doesn't stand out.

Oh no, the principal. I crouch in the middle of the scrum. I'm going to be very obvious if and when I get the chair though, and even more so when I am freewheeling it down the lanes.

"Peter Farber's new body won't walk," I say towards the nurse over the heads of all the bodies. "I was sent for the wheelchair." When the truth fits, use it.

The woman, looking like she is trapped by zombies, waves at the chair. They didn't think of getting the woman help on a day like this. They didn't think of anything.

I hear someone say, "John, the nurse needs you." As in John Kaiser the principal, he is close again. "Find Murphy," he says back, now even closer.

My mind is stricken. There is no way he won't see me manhandling the chair out the door. I'll be under arrest, then I can't help Andrew. It's all their fault. The school can't lose a student. They are going to stick me with it all. Victory for Sterling Stella, again. I close my eyes. She's on game. I grit my teeth until my jaw hurts. No, I promise. It's game on. My nose is running, and I'm crying.

Chapter Five

My fingers wrap around the wheelchair's handles. I'm not small now. The chair has made me obvious and enormous. After the principal moves down the hall, I push the wheelchair into the crowd. I run into Hannah's shins, and she glares at me. When the footrest clips Michael's Achilles' tendon, he kicks like a mule.

"Get out of the way then," I say back. "I need this for Andrew."

God, it's all like triage after a war. I see a free space, and I careen the chair into it.

I walk fast behind it, curving around obstructions in the road like a bunny running from a hawk in a debris field. I'm just about to break away, when a classroom door opens in front of me. I hit it going like ninety. The handhold of the chair punches into my stomach and winds me.

"Laura! Are you all right?" says Mrs. Lions. "Do you know the principal is looking for you?"

"He sent me after this chair for Andrew," I say in a blown-out voice.

"Andrew?"

"He's Peter Farber. He thinks he can't walk."

"My God. What a mess. I told them. When I heard about the problems at the trials. I told them. There will be a lawsuit."

I can smell cigarette smoke on her. It's like several packs strong, and an empty coffee mug in her hand. She's coping. Two boys start fighting over the water fountain. One's nose is bleeding. Mrs. Lions takes her bulk over to them, and I make a break for it.

I have no idea if Andrew is still in the chemistry room, or what I'll do if he's not. Maybe he really studied his legs and figured it out, or someone moved him. I feel a little better when I remember Peter wouldn't drag himself an inch of anywhere. He's not into exercise. *That boy has no initiative*, Gran would say.

"Thank God." The words expel from me when I see him, still on the floor. I need to get Peter-Andrew into the chair, to a door, and out. My home is only five blocks away.

"You need to get into this." Peter and I, mostly me, get him into the chair. My head is in his armpit. "God would you push up from the floor. Andrew is all legs." Which, in the situation, sounds funny to me, and I start laughing, and then I'm too weak to lift. We are sort of in status quo, no strength to go up, and he is yelling at me not to drop him and to quit laughing.

Peter's hair is standing on end from static electricity, but he is in the chair.

"Get out of my way," I call as I drive him through the hallway. Students dip or fly away. I see the exit to the great outdoors, the bright light, the pine. I can taste the fresh air, picture my liberty. I speed up. I angle towards the auto-door opener. I have to slow down to tap it, my undoing. I yell when I'm grabbed by the shoulders. I am lifted by the arms around my waist. I push at them and kick behind. "I have to help Andrew."

"Bring him," Kaiser, the evil genius who wants to destroy the world, says from behind me.

"Torture me! I don't know anything!"

"We are not going to torture you. Laura, you are our only link to her. Without you, we have no idea where to look."

~

Back in the principal's stuffy office in the tired chair, I could shoot anyone in my sight line. At least Andrew is beside me. I stand and slap my hand on the surface of Kaiser's desk. "He's Peter Farber. You assured us that that wouldn't happen."

Mr. Kaiser's eyes left me and went to Andrew. "How are you Andrew?"

"He's not Andrew, and I will not look for myself." I force out the words behind clenched teeth. Then I remember Mrs. Lions and her nerves. "I hear that the trials for this might start a lawsuit."

"Who told you that?"

"It's a riot out there."

The man stares at me and at Andrew. He is a short round man who has been ready to leave his job for years. He swivels his chair to look out the window. The light on his face shows that he wishes he had left. He is concerned, and he is out of options.

"Andrew appears to be fine. He is Andrew, of course he is. He'll, uh, be back to normal soon. Think, now, for Stella's sake, where would you go?"

"I told you, I would go home."

"We looked there."

"I wouldn't let you see me. SHE wouldn't let you see her. She is not supposed to be at my house." I shout the last bit. Nothing has happened like they said it would. Nothing.

That startles him. He draws in a long breath and lets it out quietly. He offers me and Andrew candy. I tell him I'd already had several.

No kid ever sits for long in a principal's office. It's a nervous space, not a place to lean back and reflect on the day. We are on two teams. As he tries to win me over, I ignore him. I look at a picture of his kid and then at a black-framed poster. I read the title, "Attitude," and stare at the athletic person, all fat-free and muscle floating over a high jump. I think it should be called "Altitude."

Peter-Andrew, trapped with me and by me, watches events from whatever distant planet his brain is beaming from. It is the first time in a long time Peter's DNA has inhabited a body not under the influence, and he is following the events of my life with new clarity. That's another thing Andrew and Peter don't have in common. Peter loves gossip.

Stella has taken off. The principal's brow is gutted with worry about her alone in the big, wide world of McCall, Idaho. "She always takes care of herself, you know. She has a great network."

The man eyeballs me with his strained orbs. "She may not be able to control the growth."

"Growth?"

"Some of the genes are more active than others. I don't know, dominant."

"Like schizo? Like two personalities? Like Andrew?" I remember Mrs. Lions and the trials.

He nods.

I glance at Andrew.

Kaiser sees the look. "Just in a few people." Then like he remembers that he wants me worried, he adds, "They, the few, had to be helped until the effects wore off."

Peter-Andrew's drawl slides into the break in conversation. "For Stella and Elmur here, it's like sticking the mind of a dwarf into the head of an evil queen. No, I mean, think about it, a bandy-legged, daft-headed hobbit type person into something that would eat it for breakfast rather than have a conversation with it."

I didn't know Peter was so well read.

"That's enough, Andrew," said Kaiser. "Why are you in a wheelchair?"

"It's Peter Farber, so he thinks he can't walk. His consciousness doesn't know he is in another body. You said that we would remain ourselves. You..." I lean in towards him and punch my finger at his nose. "...are scum."

"Are you scum is the question." Kaiser's eyes regard me. "Will you look for her anyway?"

He's quick on the come-back. It's ripe and smelly that he has pulled the conscience card on me. I mean he created all this. Hah.

"No. Why should I? What has she ever done for me?" I hear her in my mind saying, *What a horrible thing to say.* Even without an injection, she is always in my mind. "What has she not done to me?" I mumble while looking at my toes.

The principal's phone rings. It's jumping on top of his institutional desk, because it's also in vibration mode. It hammers like a baby woodpecker into the wood surface. The thing goes quiet at the prompt of his voice.

I wait and let my eyes gaze out the window. The snow is mushy and falls off a tree. Water drips from the roof. Drip, drip, drip. I'm suddenly tired. My stomach growls. I couldn't eat breakfast. No one is going to let me eat.

"Yes, Yes," Kaiser says to the phone, and he leaps up. "Stay here," he says to me.

Once more alone in the office, a regular event now it seems, I growl at Peter-Andrew, "How did you get to be so lucky to get Andrew?"

As if Peter can read me like a prescription bottle, which he can as I am as transparent as dried shellac, he asks, "Sore you aren't out there living the life of the evil queen?" It appears that Andrew isn't helping me out one bit, instead my best friend maybe helping.

"Yes."

Peter-Andrew wheels his chair towards the door.

"Hey, where are you going?"

34

"I'm hungry. What does Andrew eat, like nothing? They have to feed us. Let's order food."

"How?"

"He has a secretary."

"She'll bring us food?"

"If we complain enough."

Andrew would never complain. With Peter as Andrew though, we got milk, which kind of choked Peter, and cafeteria pizza with pepperoni which kind of choked Andrew until I grab the slice from Peter-Andrew's hand.

"Hey! Are you crazy?"

"You can't eat that. You can't eat any meat. It will make you sick, give you a stomach ache or worse. Right now I can't do worse, especially with you in a wheelchair thinking you can't walk. Pick the pepperoni off."

He glares at me.

"I mean it. I've never been more serious. Andrew hasn't eaten meat since he was ten."

Peter-Andrew then glares at his pizza. Maybe he doesn't get it, but he does pick off the pepperoni.

"What's is it like in there?" I tap my finger on his forehead after taking a drink.

"It's like adding a new perspective. I think maybe I will scuba-dive with sharks, maybe Elmur is too obsessed with herself." He bobs his head and flashes gorgeous a smile. Andrew doesn't use that feature quite as well. "Just being a new me."

Whose new perspective that comes from I can't tell. I sulk over my straw. I could be running amok out in the halls with my own new perspective; flying from one person to the next, while saying the wittiest things and everyone crowding me. Instead, I am eating no longer frozen pizza in lock down with a remix of my life-long friend Andrew. *Shoot me now.*

I put my feet up on the chair and wrap my arms around my bent legs. Peter-Andrew is eating like a starving child. It's probably been awhile since he's really tasted food.

He pokes me with half of his brownie.

I'm not sure I want it, this offer of kindness, maybe because I'm mad at both of them. Maybe I just want to sit in my wrapped sorrows. It's a kind of achievement, getting through life the hard way. I want points for not being special and still showing up.

Peter-Andrew shrugs. Nothing like a take-back offer to change a mind. I know it's really Andrew offering. It is chocolate after all.

"So, what if I don't go looking for her? Even if I do, what if I can't find her? Look at you, the dominant perspective. She's more herself than me."

I stand up and go to the window. The spring day is changing, clouding up. If she can't control the mind buzz, she could be out in the dropping temperatures. We are at five thousand feet. Maybe she did go crazy. Naw.

"I've never been able to best her. Wherever she is, it's beyond me to find her. She stayed on top for sure. I'll just tell them that. They can go to missing persons, her mother, her best friends." I sigh as the first raindrops hit the window. "She wouldn't do it for me."

Peter-Andrew is wiping off his mouth with his napkin, and then he uses a clean one for his fingers. The exercise in cleanliness reminds me of Andrew who brushes his teeth and flosses after eating a peanut. Andrew is in there somewhere. I wonder what Andrew is thinking of all this in the crowded space of his own brain. Now that it's happened to him, and he's not crazy, maybe he's finding it very Frankenstein. Andrew doesn't dislike people like he says I do, and he does like the idea of Frankenstein. It's all like a hard knot in my gut.

The Principal's glare rejoins us. He's not even fake-smiling now. He threads around my chair and Peter-Andrew's until he reaches his spot. As he sits, he unbuttons his suit jacket. His tie rests on the desk, and he smooths it down along the line of his white shirt.

"Have you been thinking?"

"Yes, I've been thinking that she is more herself than me."

"Just think for yourself. Forget about Stella," says Kaiser.

"I just don't…"

"Anything."

"I mean, you've already checked my house, my room."

My room. She could have been my room laughing at my French provincial canopy bed or my zodiac poster or Zee Zee the fat zebra. Where's my blanket! It doesn't matter where it is. She knows that I hide things; that I'm jealous and angry a lot; that I dislike people and don't want to; that I'm shy and sensitive. She senses I can't stand to be embarrassed, and I can't watch others be embarrassed. She knows all my shame points. I put my hands over my face, and I sob, because I can't stop it, because I feel like the inside privacy of me no longer exists.

When my disconsolation eases, I stand. "I am taking Andrew home. If she shows, if I think of anything, I'll be sure to call forthwith." I need a desolate space that will cover me and hide me. That's what I do. I hide. I'm just being true to myself.

"Let me find someone to help us," the principal says as he goes back out into the melee.

He needs time for some new persuasional words, because he can't let me go, because I'm all he has in his desperate time. Feel sorry for him, *not*.

After some time, when no one reopens the door, I creep to it and press my ear to the wood and listen. "It's very quiet."

As I turn the knob, I press on the panel. I open the door by milligrams, and peer out with one googly eye. Beyond the inner sanctum of the office, the hall is scarce with bodies.

"The secretaries' area is eerily empty," I whisper to Peter-Andrew. "Maybe the zombie-students are now in control of the school, and they have taken them all away and have eaten them." That's one way to get out of here.

Chapter Six

I open the door of Principal Kaiser's office, wide open, to an empty room of secretaries' desks and personal computers. I don't step over the threshold. I'm certain that if I do, if I move even a toe past the door jam, some alien head that looks like Mrs. Brain will play whack-a-mole with me, and I don't have a mallet to hit back. Creepy alien moles.

I'm also not moving because it's disturbing, no people where there is supposed to be half a dozen. I have in front of me a really empty office. A computer with a lit screen and nobody looking at it. A chair is pushed way back, as in hastily, some papers on the floor. Maybe the injected genes carried a mutant virus, and Peter-Andrew and I are the last two living beings in the building. I mean, I'm hopeful, as I wait on my glued feet.

I hear the nurse yell at some leftover, mixed-up kid, so no such luck. I decide that what I have in front of me though is pure opportunity. I'll e-mail Mr. Kaiser my: where-would-I-go-if-I-was-knocking-souls-in-the-body-of-Stella list.

As I move into the office area, my skin tingles, waiting for someone to step out of the woodwork. They have closed the door to the main area of the school. That door is never closed. I have the sinking feeling that it is the locked door.

"The nurse's station. Go that way," suggests Peter-Andrew who has rolled up behind me.

I shake my head. "They'll have told her to watch for a tall kid in a wheelchair and a short kid pushing it. We are obvious, How about this, you stand up and WALK out with me."

"Not until Christmas I don't."

"You need a miracle."

Or a decent wizard would go down good right about now.

I try the door. It is dead-bolted shut. *Shenanigans*. "Isn't this a fire hazard, that I can't open it from the inside without a key?" I gaze at Peter-Andrew, and he gazes at me. "You start looking over there. They didn't all take their keys," I say. "Hurry, it's not like we have all day. Gotta be drawers, they walk in take off their coats, walk to their desks, open a drawer, drop in the keys." Peter-Andrew is opening the secretaries' desk drawers or the Peter in him is opening them. Andrew would never. Peter shakes something. I hear the jingle and turn.

"And something else," he says. He looks down. I walk around the desk and look into the box that he is holding open. "Our phones."

"You are fantastical."

I dig out mine and Andrew's and Peter's. So satisfying. Then I try to grab the key ring, but he yanks them from my vicinity. I grab his arm in both my hands. He laughs and lets them drop to the floor. I shake him.

"God, Elmur. Lighten up."

"Pig."

"Cow."

I bend down to grab the keys. Peter-Andrew pops the wheel of the chair like he is going to run over me. Bottom feeder. I try two keys. With the third, I'm wondering if this ring will help me. With the fourth, I wonder if we will be going home at all. With the fifth, I mutter, "Who has this many forsaken keys?" But then I hear the sweet sound of the bolt turning. Sheeerlock. I yank the door open, and then stomp down on the door jam. I hurry to Peter-Andrew and take the wheelchair by the handholds. Peter is fighting me by grabbing the wheels.

"You're going."

"You're not my mommy."

"Why did you help then?"

"Why do you think?"

"Come on, Andrew, help me."

With me pushing and him holding, the wheels slide about two inches across the linoleum floor. "Ok, ok, ok." I say. "It's not like I want to listen to you call me dwarf." I retrace my steps to the hallway and check both ways. "Only I promised YOU, Andrew, that we would look out for each other, a blood promise."

"Woo, a blood promise."

"You know…" I shake the wheelchair. "You, Peter, are used, bargain-brand toilet paper." I want to turn Peter-Andrew upside down to shake out Pumpkin Eater. I give the chair one more shove. "Do you really want to stay here, Peter? You leave school all the time."

Peter-Andrew shrugs his shoulders. "Sticking with you is risky. Stella is out to curse you. Battle of the giant squid and the shrimp. Giant squid eat shrimp. How fast can shrimp swim?"

"Pretty darn fast. Swim team."

I stare at the shell of my friend. *Where are you in there, Andrew? How can you let him*…ah, fuhgeddaboudit. I kick the tire of the chair so hard that it turns. I grab the handles and tip Peter-Andrew back onto the two big wheels. Now, he feels like he is falling. I run through the office door, and I hit the wheelchair button at a run. As the front doors crack open, Peter-Andrew is yelling that he's being abducted. To force the chair back on its front wheels, he throws his body forward from the waist. I am so done with all this, still, when the two front wheels hit the ground, I've already gotten him out. We are over the threshold. He is poised again for mutiny, another grab at the wheels. Idiot. They should have done this experiment to us in kindergarten. All the important lessons in life are learned by the age of five.

"If you touch that wheel, I will tie your hands."

"With what?" he says, but he lets me push.

And then it starts to sleet. *Perfect.* The wheelchair toboggans like a sled.

"I'm a popsicle here," he calls. "You're taking care of me remember?"

"I call shenanigans." I have to stop for a second. Get my breath. It's uphill to my house. In a mountain town, everything is always uphill to some degree. I pant next to the twigs of Mrs. Amberley's leafless rosebush. I push on, but at the lip of the hill, just before the flat, I begin to slip backwards. I dig my shoes into the wet, but there is no purchase. The school is sucking me back. The chair is over running my body, and then I hear a voice from the sky.

"Necessitas help chicatita?"

God has a Spanish accent.

"Hey ya there Hugo," Peter-Andrew drawls. "Did Kaiser send you for me?"

I'd only gotten Peter-Andrew four blocks away from school. Comical, bank robbers have better get-a-ways.

I've never been so close to Hugo Sanchez. It's like being at the feet of a copper-brown statue, the sympathetic, carved face, the height, and the solidness. You could trip on the granite of Hugo's long, tennis shoe. His jawbone, a real treat to a pack of dogs, is in perfect harmony to his bruiser biceps and wide eyes. If I'm a schnauzer to Andrew's Great Dane, I'm a teacup Yorkie to Hugo's Saint Bernard, a Saint Bernard with dreadlocks. Hugo is the not the runt of his litter. He's like Clifford the Dog, all the love made him grow and grow. I see his family at his football games, all six of them, every game, minus his dad. I don't know which genes he grabbed, but he is big for his age, his race, his everything.

He's not just called Hugo. He's called 'Hey you Huge-o.'

We lost thirty-six straight games before he arrived. He likes black leather jackets and keeps his hair long. He's already ready for the NFL.

I heard his mother went to the Olympics for Mexico in ice-skating. She didn't win or even come close but got lots of press for being a first. The local rink was excited to get an Olympian of any stature for their ice-skating program. I skated there once. Gran made me wear a helmet. She doesn't like hospitals.

"I got it." This big guy who enjoys such great personal branding says. Nudging me aside, Hugo grips the wheelchair. He pushes it uphill not down like I was recently doing. He manages it like it is a doll stroller.

"Where to?" Hugo says.

"You aren't here to take Andrew back?"

"You looked like you needed help."

If he does orchestrate an about-turn and rolls Andrew back, there is nothing I can do to stop him. On my own, I was sliding back towards the school anyway. Hugo is a stereotypical big guy, acres of muscle and heart. He plays football like that, always helping up the guy he has just mowed over, always going out of his way to pat the guy on the back that made the great play, even on the other team. Gran and I and Andrew go to all the football games. It's something to do here, and Andrew loves football because it's a real-time game in which people get to wear armor and push each other around on a field of battle. He'd even play if he got to hold a weapon and got to wear face paint. Of course, football-loving Gran, with Andrew, thinks Hugo lives by the warrior's code.

"It's Gran's bowling day, and I have to go home and see if she's been there," I say because I have no idea why.

Closer in to ground zero, my house. Hugo leaves me with Andrew as he does a walk by. "There is nobody. I don't think that they know you are gone yet."

"Que lastima!" says Andrew using his high school Spanish. So that's when he makes the effort! He couldn't help himself. He loves, loves Spanish. Bet he had a mental wrestle with Peter over those words.

"Let's go in the back anyway, just in case."

Usually, only the expensive lake-front houses here have fences, to keep people out. My neighborhood is a beehive of small houses without landscaping, or rather natural landscaping. It's cheaper and takes care of itself. The lots were carved out of the forest, and nobody added much to the pines and brush that had been left between houses. The sleet is turning to rain. I manhandle the chair through the door, and Hugo carries Peter-Andrew, who has quit squawking probably because he is beginning to enjoy the game.

I pop the chair over the lip of the back door. I hold the screen for Hugo. As he passes, his arm is in my face, and I inhale damp wool from his jacket.

My dog, Damsel, arrives and runs circles around us, and barks. I pick up her seven pounds of white fluff and rub her belly.

"Who's a great girl? Who's a great girl?" I put her down. "Wait here, and I'll get towels. Take off your shoes." I thread through the house wondering if I will be able to find clean towels or something like clean.

My Gran is old, the house is old, and the furniture is old. There is a lack of brand-new air in the place. I mean it's great for Andrew and me. At one time the house and everything in it including Gran had color, but now it's all too ancient to care. What was once brown is now taupe, what was red, taupe, orange, taupe. It's easier on Gran's cataracts. With those, she sees our lives as a blurry brown.

"Gran," I call in case someone has gotten her home early. I glance at her armchair in front of the television. The sag in the cushion is Gran-less. If Kaiser has her captive and sitting upright in his hard seat on her hemorrhoids, she won't be happy. Where do you think your granddaughter has gone? Funny, I am right where I said I would be. *Stupid people.*

I pick some hardly used towels from the floor of the

bathroom. When the guys are drier, I lead them towards my room. Hugo, Peter-Andrew, me, huddle at the closed door. I push the door for a slow reveal, like if I see something lunge, I can slam it shut. When he can see inside, Peter-Andrew says, "My brother has a cleaner car, and we call it The Toilet."

My hand flies to my gaping mouth. The bedroom has been ransacked. "I told Mr. Kaiser I'd come home first." The words explode from my solar plexus, and then my heart stops. Sterling Stella was looking for something, something incriminating, something, anything, to make my life not worth living.

Chapter Seven

Somebody, I dunno, maybe one of the books that Gran buys me, says that self-pity comes from the selfishness of being too self-absorbed or self-important. If that is thinking about how people have done me wrong, then right now self-pity is giving me a second wind to shove the bed back into place and then pile onto it, from the floor, sheets and blankets.

I pick up ZeeZee, the round stuffed zebra with two poke-out ears that always sits next to my pillow; the stuffed animal that this morning before school I put on and then took off my bed a billion times. I decided to leave it on, nobody was supposed to be in my room, and ZeeZee's feelings would be hurt if I stuck her in the closet. She would be insulted to be next to stuff like all the virtual games for math and grammar improvement that Gran bought me. Spelling frogs that leap at the sound of a correct letter and croak at a wrong one. If that frog opened its mouth one more time it was gonna be one dead reptile.

Gran has always been trying. "I don't know why you came to me," she always says. "Obviously, I didn't do too well the first time." I tell her practice makes perfect. Neither of us really believes it though. The googly eyes of the spelling frog are glazed with dust.

I squash the zebra against me as I touch the wall near the closet that Sterling Stella egged. She did an award-winning job on the room, mostly on my zodiac poster that says I'm special. The word 'love' is dripping yolk.

"You've got to be kidding me," Peter-Andrew says from the door.

"I hate her." I clutch Zee Zee closer as I sit on my bed. I can feel sadness, anger and that useless self-pity crawl up the lining of my throat like a nest of red ants. Just in case, because I didn't really believe the adults, I had cleaned this room, down to the last deck of cards on my shelves for that person who would be me. I had put treasured items, the things that I knew were just too young for me now, but were still out in my room into boxes, like the stuffed cow that had been in my baby crib that when its legs were pulled played "Twinkle, Twinkle, Little Star and my blankie. It is all about image, everyone knows that. I had sanitized mine.

I remember taking down my favorite childhood book, my first Easter bunny, my first lost tooth and placing them into covered darkness. It seemed to me that trying to brand myself didn't involve teeth. I had dusted under the bed. For this person. FOR THIS PERSON, just in case.

Peter-Andrew rolls his chair over my clean underwear that is on the floor that had been carefully folded and put into the drawer by color.

"Why would anyone, anyone do this? What gives her the right to do this?" I say as I jump up and tug some purple briefs out from under his tire.

"Has she stolen anything?" asked Hugo.

"Would those be dragon statutes?" Peter asks as he is staring at my shelf of mystical beings.

I cringe that my branding efforts weren't as good as I thought.

"Maybe she was looking for something," suggests Hugo.

"She doesn't want any of my stuff. She wants to show me what she thinks of it and me, because she can, because she always has." I sit on the edge of my bed again. "She's not looking for anything. She's me…remember? Why would she be looking? She should be able to saunter right to it."

"Maybe the blending isn't that clear. Maybe you're keeping stuff from her."

"Great job me then." I begin picking up clothes. Hugo helps. "She makes people laugh at me. All the time. Everyone thinks she's so friendly and kind. It's an act." I grab my trashcan and drop slivers of eggshells into it. "Friendly and kind my foot."

"I'd see if anything is missing, eh?"

"How? Her room is all over the place," says Peter-Andrew.

I walk over and reach up and pull the tacks from my poster. A birthday present. Gran is always trying to help me like myself better. I ease it from the wall, a drop of yoke falls onto my arm. It's like my veins are being yanked and my ventricles are tearing. I put my hand over my mouth and, grit my teeth against the pain. It is lonely and really hurtful to see your bedroom whacked with eggs. It's worse than being the last person picked for a line. It's more violent.

My poster is ruined. I clench my fist as my insides squeeze, and I smack the wall hard. I grunt at the blow and the pain stuns my system. I shake my hand. When Gran sees the hole, she is going to buy me inflatable, boxing gloves to work on my anger issues, which I will need as it occurs to me that right now there are two of me beating me up. One of us has to cease and desist. I glare at the hole where smooth wall had been. There's no fixing it without a scar, a forever blemish from the day I was egged.

Peter is leaning over the armrest of his chair to pick up a pile of bras. I grab them from him. Hugo hands me a rainbow of shirts. I shove the clothes into an open drawer. I squash them in and then force the drawer shut. "She wants me to know she's been here, and that she doesn't like…hates being me. No news there. She wants me to be afraid."

"I agree with Hugo. The feeling that something is gone, is an itch on my nose," says Peter-Andrew. "She took something, I'm telling you."

"Found what she was looking for."

"What would that be?" Peter asks.

I glance around the mess. I stare at the closet and then leap over old gaming boxes that litter the floor. I toss learning-support stuff aside. "Where's my box?" I shovel through the clothes in my closet. I crouch down sifting through the debris. On my haunches, I see it, grab it, and open it.

"It's empty." I shake it upside down, hoping that what is not there might magically fall out anyway. I remember that I moved it to a safer harbor.

Hearing a circulating pulse in my brain. I push into my closet and yank open a smaller door there. I thump up the narrow stairs. As my head passes the threshold of the floor, I note the change in temperature. The attic area is cold. I smell my private incense of dust and old insulation. I painted the stairs in a black and white checkerboard. Andrew and I had written favorite quotes on the red walls of the stairwell. Pausing, I note that the area has not been shaken down. Ok, then, maybe the worst hasn't happened. I finish moving up the stairs. I crawl to a plywood platform. On top of it is furniture that Andrew and I got curbside—a futon that's mattress had gone hard, a table with two legs that leans against the angle of the roof, a disembodied medicine cabinet and mirror, an old gaming station paired with a flat screen television. I get all Gran's old TV's. She keeps up with the latest models.

I move plates with molded food and candy wrappers so I can lie flat on a colorless carpet and reach deep into a space under the rafters. My hand pats down the area. My forehead is on the carpet, my nose is breathing in dust. Hugo was right. She knew that it existed, but she didn't know where to find it. When I saw the attic intact, hope had flared. Maybe she hadn't been able to find it or hadn't wanted to stick her hand into a rafter that had mice droppings all around it. Maybe that's why she egged my room.

Nah, she didn't find it. I wouldn't let her know where it is.

Still, my hand pats the narrow space. I pull myself forward a little more and angle my head into the place between the roof of the house and the floor of the attic, and I peer into the corner with one eye. All the good feelings evaporate. It is gone. Her mind had evidently taken mine by storm.

I drop, leg upon leg, back down the stairs until my feet are once again in the litter of the closet. The boys crane their necks around the corner of the closet doors. "She came looking," I say. "While she searched, she brutalized my things until, I bet, something triggered."

"What did she get from up there?" asks Hugo.

"It's your diary isn't it?" Peter-Andrew says.

I gaze at my friend, or through him, or into him. What it is like to have the self-consciences of two difference people. I'll never know. The President of the Unites States told us on the video chat that all brain cells have a full set of genes, but only some genes are expressed at a time. Different genes pop into action in different places. So Peter-Andrew is in my home, in my room. In this place, Andrew's genes, his memories are calling out. Stella has my diary. Now she has some of me in her mind and all of me written down on paper. The rest is going to be all her.

As if to prove the President right, Peter-Andrew mixes it up. "Elmur—" *Andrew never calls me Elmur.* "—writes everything down. Like, you know, when you write down what you want to do to people and what you think of them, but THEN, you're supposed to *burn it*."

I half stick my tongue out at him.

"It wasn't going places. Only here."

Peter sneezes the word, "Stupid." Hugo slugs his shoulder.

Peter-Andrew wheels towards the door. "Come on, Laura, let's get some tea and chocolate, or hot chocolate. You have to make it."

When I'm upset, I have tea and chocolate. When I'm really upset, I cook. I'm a specialist at hot chocolate. In the middle of my mess, Hugo takes my hand and pulls me out the door. He closes it.

I open a kitchen cupboard and take out cocoa, salt, and sugar. Hugo looks for a pan. I add hot water and heat it until it boils. When it boils, I add the milk and heat it back up. It can't boil again. If it boils, the milk and chocolate structure will change. I take it off the stove and add vanilla and a little cinnamon.

As I pour it into mugs, I think how too much heat can ruin things. I don't know why milk is delicate and not water. Milk is partially water. I am milk. Andrew, Hugo, even Peter, they are water. Stella is water. Water boils. Milk bubbles and overflows the pan. That's me. I am milk, and they are water.

Peter-Andrew says great job on the hot chocolate after I give it to him, and he takes a drink. I like the compliment, even more, for some reason, with the sound of Peter's drawl in it. Compliments are good.

"Line of scrimmage, no split end," Hugo repeats when I hand him a cup.

"I don't get it," I reply.

"It appears like you are out of options."

"Ya. You got any ideas on where to hide away till things blow over? Your house?"

"Ah, no. No ganas. You want to win this game?"

"There is no game. There is just me and Peter-Andrew laying low."

"Stella is at this moment devising a plan to crush you. Kaiser is correct. You have to find her."

"To do what?"

"Beat her at her own game."

"Oh ya, because I've been so close to ever doing that."

"People say it is because of me that we win games. You can't win a game alone. And it's the new coach. He was the first to unbalance his front line by moving his split end and by using a no-huddle snap. It worked because it is new. You too must be nuevo. What we want to do is make her go where you want her to go. Misdirection. Deception, eh?"

"Okaaaayyyy?"

"You need to lead. You need to run past the people who want to hold you back. The thing is, you are more yourself than Stella is. You will be able to see things faster...see a pattern."

"Is that what Mr. Kaiser told you to say, Hugo?"

I want to take my chocolate delights right out of his mouth, and then I see the pain on his face.

When Hugo is on the field, he never fakes an injury. Our team used to have another really good player, Robert B. In every game Robert B, at least once, laid on the field clutching his ankle or thigh or whatever. The game stopped, and the physical therapists ran out, and fussed, and inspected, and then helped Robert B off the field, his arms draped over their shoulders. Robert B was never sidelined long, a few plays. He got better so quickly. Not Hugo. Honest. If "The Big Guy" is here for Kaiser he'd say so.

"I'm sorry. I say stupid things all the time. My modus operando. I'm more defensive than offensive."

Peter-Andrew laughs, and Hugo chuckles.

"What?" My face squishes into a frown.

"Offensive? Offensive," says Peter-Andrew.

"Ok, yeah, I get it."

"Come on, you gotta laugh."

"I do?"

"Yeah. Yeah Elmur, sometimes you do."

"We can play defense if you want. Defense has plays of its own. It's not just read 'em and weep. It's aggressive. Sack the quarterback." He winks at me.

"I'd love to sack the hell out of her. It can't be done." I grab a part of the wheelchair to pull myself up to my feet from the floor in front of a pellet fire. Hugo and I move furniture to make a path for Peter-Andrew, and I see the nicer, cleaner carpet where the sofa had been. I brush my drying jeans and orange sweatshirt of crumbs. "If you don't have an arm, you don't box."

"Unless you get the other guy's arm pinned behind his back."

"Or if someone has your back."

"Who has my back? Hey Peter, walk for the man." I tap my index finger on the side of my head. "He thinks his legs are still mending. That gets team Murphy down to one."

It doesn't seem to bother The Big Guy that the Peter-Andrew part of our team is inhabited, or haunted or conquered by stronger genes; or that I didn't say or think that he is really on my team. The Big Guy just drinks more chocolate.

"Why do you want to help me?"

"Because you're a tackle that is dragged yards downfield. You don't let go."

"Is that a compliment? I guess. How do you see that anyway?"

Hugo gets up and wraps me into a hug that I can't see out of.

"Give me one good reason to look for her," my muffled voice says. I'm not used to being hugged. It makes me all fierce terrier, show no weakness. Andrew is not a hugger, or Gran. Not being used to them, I'm not sure I like hugs. They're awkward and confining, I'm claustrophobic. I can hear his heart and that is weird.

He releases me, and I notice that there is a kind of warmth from him that evaporates.

"This time, she has gone too far," he says to me then.

"Sure, Hugo, it sounds good, and I want to because I should never give in, but Andrew is presently residing in his big toe, and Peter's been great...not. Basically, no thanks. Even with you. I don't think we can ganamos."

Chapter Eight

Sirens split the air. Emergency vehicles speed past the house. The noise gathers and then diminishes in waves as each vehicle passes. My ears track the sound.

In a dash to a window, I slip on some magazines on the floor. Hugo gets to the window first and says, "There's smoke. Lots of it." He yanks Peter's chair around and speeds him out the door. Gran's has always been my safety house. I take in the open door. I think that I should just go back and start cleaning up the first mess from all this before the next one crops up. I know that all this sound is because of her. The light through the door is so bright, the clouds are lifting. Oh well, my bedroom looks like an explosion most of the time anyway. Maybe her fingerprints are on the eggshells. If I'm protecting Andrew, he's gone.

Outside, Peter-Andrew and Hugo stare at a tar-black column rising in the sky. It's at least three miles away.

"Come on, rapidamento." Hugo says.

The black particles in the sky boil like a demon's rage. We have to get there.

"Over here." I spring to the garage. I punch in a code and hear the swish of the door as it opens automatically. I grab one of two electrified push-scooters. These are Andrew-built. To the body of a long board, for speed, are attached by PVC pipes two all-terrain tires. The scooters have aging lithium batteries tied onto the back of twelve inches of board. Electric motors are attached to a racing curve off the end of the platform. They go twenty mph with disc brakes that work off of a kill switch on the handlebars mounted on a PVC pole in front. I unplug one scooter and then I smack my head with my palm as I remember Peter. I pause, tapping my fingers on the handlebar. I hear them behind me, Hugo pushing Peter into the garage. Their voices pause, and I know that they are waiting, watching me. I wheel scooter-one to the front. I leave it with Hugo and then return with a rope, one end of which I put into the big guys hands. The skateboards have a second pole mounted just in front of the battery with a bike seat to sit upon for long trips.

"It's like waterskiing," I say as with fierce tugs I knot the rope onto the seat-pole. Hugo glances at the rope he holds and then back at me. "Ease out the length and tie it to Andrew's chair. I'll ride the scooter. I'm lighter, you know for the engine. I'll take up the slack, and then when it's taunt, increase speed, so more like road-skiing."

I'm not sure if it will be Andrew or Peter who won't let The Big Guy tie it to the chair. I'm about to start my convincing speech, when I notice a crazy smile is spreading across Peter-Andrew's face, like we have just handed him fireworks in an illegal state. There's no tie-off. Peter-Andrew's got the excesses rope on his lap. The rest is wrapped around the fists of his hands. He really is ready to ski.

"I'll go SLOW," I say, but it's like talking to a puppy whose head is out a car window. "I'll be careful," I say to the Andrew part. I can't figure why he isn't speaking up. Andrew would never in a million years let me do this. After getting Hugo going on the other scooter, I start my wheels and roll forward and Peter's chair reacts, which scares me enough that I hit the brakes. My hands are sweating. I begin again, and we are moving sort of faster—like a slug that has just smelled salt. Peter is throwing his weight and whooping. Ooooh…kaaay. I press for more speed.

Andrew and I are not daring people. I don't jump off of even the short cliff into the lake. I hate roller coasters and heights. I get carsick. Andrew refuses to tilt-a-whirl. His mother calls us Safe and Safer. If people were meant to jump off of things, we'd look more like cats. Next thing I know, Peter's done a face plant. His pant leg at the knee is gone, his face is gravel speckled. The chair yanks me. I fall off the scooter but manage to press the stop button before the chair drags Peter's head. He's moaning from the part of him that is Andrew. My friend is gonna kill me. I'll blame Peter. He's the guy driving the chair. Hugo is there to roll him over, and Peter spits dirt.

"Got all your teeth, hombre?" Hugo asks.

"My legs," Peter-Andrew says.

"They're still there, dude." I say. Although I remember that Andrew and I promised we'd look after each other. I now feel the pull of the smoke. I can smell it. The taint of its acidity is in my mouth. He's patted down his legs, and still isn't walking. His gene cocktail seems to make him more stupid. Anyway, he's dusty and rock speckled, but Hugo has him back in his seat, and he, himself has taken the rope back in his hands. My eyebrows lift. Why not? Why not. Looking over my shoulder, I take up the slack of the rope again.

The second time I dump Andrew, I'm expecting him to yell that he's being kidnapped. Eventually, I'm towing the chair, and Peter is learning to let go when he's about to eat dirt. I don't know how we make it. We probably could've walked faster. Andrew's face would've look better.

When our parade rounds the final corner, ash is falling on us. Over blackening grass, fire is trying to cremate the words of the sign of a lake-front condominium, 'Blue Water Haven.' Under the sign, a fake stone fountain bubbles and spits water as burning bits dive into it. I inhale the smoke like perfume. I raise my hands to touch the heat from the blaze. I want to dance as the flames are dancing. *It is burning,* I think. *It is burning.* I pirouette. As the letters scar, I smile. The heat warms me. I have wanted to torch that sign for all my life…forever. Stella has done it. She is doubly satisfied, or not, because in the glow, I am almost grateful to her.

The wood from the sign smolders, pops and sizzles like steak night on good-grades day. It's a sadness when the firemen turn on the hoses. The water washes the road. Dirt on the tarmac smells wet. A cop car's red lights revolve round and round, the color flushing Hugo's face with pink. I'd forgotten I wasn't alone.

"Let's vamanos."

"Why?"

"Because you are doing a dance of joy. Because you are like a pyro returned to the scene to watch," says Peter-Andrew.

"And that arrow," adds Hugo.

"What arrow?"

"The one sticking out of the tree next to the sign that is burning," says Peter-Andrew.

The twitch in my eye pulses with the flip-flop of my heart. There is a paper stuck on a branch on a tree, like an ugly Christmas ornament. I glance around at the cops, at the fireman, at the crowd. I check my movements, even as I say, "Could be anyone's arrow." I know it's mine though, stolen from my room. So does my team.

"It needed fuel to torch like that," Peter-Andrew observes.

"Probably that." Hugo points to a red plastic sand bucket, my old red plastic sand bucket.

"You are right. She has gone too far." I am mesmerized by the blistering, painted letters.

Peter pulls on my coat sleeve. "That paper's got a jagged edge, like it's been torn, like from a diary, Elmur," Peter-Andrew says.

All I had wanted from this day were a few months as a person who isn't weighed down by the fallout of their every single syllable. All I wanted from my guest genes is a voice in my head that says to me sometimes, you're wonderful.

Best thing to do with bullies is ignore them, Gran says. But as the heat of the flames warms my face, I realize that ignoring Stella will not be enough. It's my natural inclination, but I don't want to go to jail. First, I am going to find Andrew a safe place to finish out being Peter. I don't know if that's his place or mine, or somewhere in between. I grab the handles of the wheelchair. Because I am pushing an invalid, the flood of people who are staring at the spring waterfall-load of water pelting the sign, part like we are important.

"No!" He grabs the wheels.

"Cut it out."

"We have to get the piece of paper and the bucket."

"What?" His words smack me. I quit pushing. I collapse on the curb next to the chair. I'm new to crime. "My fingerprints," I say with my head in my hands.

"Tip me over."

"What," I say again like I'm an echo of myself.

"Look, that cop has picked up the bucket. He doesn't know what he's got yet. You and Hugo tip me over by the curb next to him. NOW before he like smells it or something. Elmur, you can't pick me up right? Remember that and act it out like your life depends on it. With any luck, he'll put the bucket down. Hugo, while we are making a scene see if you can get the arrow or at least the paper. If you can get them into the fire, so much the better.

"No, the firemen are all over the fire. I'll keep it, and we can burn it later.

"They'll cop-on if the bucket disappears."

"Look at me, Elmur. I'm already all scratched up. I'll play my part. Be ready."

"How do I even get the bucket?"

"Just get out of the way so they can pick me up. Back-off next to the bucket."

I wet a handful of paper trash in the pools of water from the fire hoses. "I'll just wash my prints off it and leave it there."

I let Hugo get into place, and then I tip Peter-Andrew over the curb. I scream. His head hits grass and then he squirms until he's over pavement and face down. He's a real loud moaner.

"Oh my God, Andrew, are you alright?" I yell. "Are you ok? God, hang on. Somebody help!"

The cop looks our way. I must make it more emergency-looking. "He's a quadriplegic. I'm not sure he can breathe." I smile to myself as both cops come over then. Bonus, they bring the bucket with them as they scurry over and drop to their knees. They have to dead-man Andrew and all of his legs. Peter-Andrew is like a sack of cement with exceedingly long appendages. I crouch like I want to help, and the grab the bucket. Holding it with my t-shirt, I wipe it with the wet paper inside and out and the handle. I could be wiping away Stella's prints, but more than likely she thought of gloves. I can't let this bucket be traced back to me. Lots of red buckets in the world, only one with my prints on it. Andrew is in his chair, but he is coughing like he's about to lose his left lung.

"We'll take you to the hospital," says a cop.

"No, I'm ok." Cough, cough, and ten more coughs. "Just give me a minute."

"I think we should take you, son."

"No really, this happens a lot when I'm with her, cough. If I went every time, it would cost my mom a fortune, hack, hack."

"We'll take you home then."

"You're too busy."

Hugo enters stage left. "I can help, Officer. I know them from school. Get that fire out."

I follow the chair, thanking the cops for the saviors they

are. We did it. We are so good. I'm nearly skipping in back of the chair, then *smack*, it hits me. At the edge of the crowd, we can't leave without the scooters, and the cops are watching, no more scraping Andrew along the pavement.

"I'll bring them in a minute," Hugo says behind me. "Wait behind the grocery store."

When Hugo arrives with the second scooter, I pick up the rope. I can't bring myself to hand it to Andrew. He's been through so much.

"I've been thinking about that," says team-member Hugo. "Put one of them under the chair. He can drive it himself. See." Hugo removes the seat on the scooter and then shoves the scooter between the two big wheels of the wheelchair. He lashes the rope to the chair and to the underbelly of the scooter. It looks like an improvised electronic grocery-shoppers cart for poor Medicare patients. Before I yell the all clear, Peter-Andrew pushes the start button. He leans over the t-bar, his elbows out, his back hunched. He has the silhouette of an alien grasshopper riding a junkyard earth-vehicle.

Andrew may not be a risk taker, but he is a driver. There's no risk in skill he always says. Once he put wheels on a bathtub that he'd found. That day began the bathroom derby with first prize being a toilet brush shaped chocolate cake that his mom makes every year.

Andrew-scooters, even with the chair attached, can take a hill at a knee-skinning clip. Andrew's house is at the farthest corner of town away from mine, up the road to the little ski hill and then across. It overlooks the lake. It is in a subdivision that has roads, curbs, and fire hydrants but only a handful of houses. It's a good choice. His mom is never home. She runs and then bikes and then runs some more. She drinks lots of energy drinks that do seem to give her lots of momentum. She talks like she fears silence. He's happy to be taking his scooter home. There are four places in Andrew's world, my room, his room, the chemistry lab, and his shed.

With Andrew off-off-and-away, Hugo hands me the other scooter.

"I'll catch up to you."

Sure, I think. Things are getting hot, time to get out. "Ya, thanks," I say. "You've been more than helpful. Andrew is in charge now. He's going home. He lives in the log house in Kings Point Overlook. See ya there." *Or not.* I grab my scooter and open the throttle up to catch the wheelchair-man. With only me and Peter-Andrew heading home, let's just say that the fat lady has sung. I'm thinking, *where to hide so the next thing can't find me.* One problem, I think she plans to flush me out.

Chapter Nine

Hugo has no obligations to Andrew and me. Under pressure, Team Elmur is down one. So that means one and half of one left. No matter what Hugo says, in my world that means I'm thinking of giving up, and I know where to do it. I de-couple Peter-Andrew from his scooter, and I drag the wheelchair backwards on a wet narrow dirt path behind Andrew's house.

Huckleberry bushes and mountain rose grab at us both. Peter-Andrew pulls his sweater over his knuckles and uses his forearms to push back branches. It's about forty feet to an old pioneer cabin that has fossilized to a concrete silver. Years ago, it began leaning on its bones like an old man, and then it petrified at that angle. It's a one-roomer and the roof is low because, over one hundred or more years, dirt has filled in and around it. At age eleven, after shooing out the snakes and black widows, Andrew built a door and attached a combination lock onto it. Only he and I know the numbers. It's always been just Andrew and me.

This is the place Andrew brings and then melds the stuff he picks up from garbage dumps. Yup, Frankenstein complex. In front of a long, makeshift closet, I pile onto the uneven floor a laser fire starter, and a tent, well an Andrew tent. He sewed it from a patchwork of materials and threaded it through with fine wires that hook to a solar energy thingy. The wires connect to an LED light at the top of the tent. They feed electricity into a couple of sockets, one for his charger and one for his Easy Bake oven. He found the oven in an attic of an ancient house that was scheduled to be demolished because of blight. When camping, we eat a boat-load of chocolate cupcakes. The current is strong enough for his electric coil— ta-da, boiling water. We like tea with our cakes.

If he were totally with us now, Andrew would be screaming at the lack of ceremony as I drop his babies onto the ground. Best he can do now is a low-pitched moan coming from his throat area.

"We have to go someplace for a while to think," I say to him. "I can't go home yet, and your mother is going to return sometime and then she'll be on us like an over-sugared puppy." I look at him, give him my smiley face. "Love her," I say.

I stuff everything in three backpacks. From the cabin, it's just a half mile down a dirt path, and I mean down, that has rocks of different sizes, gigantic, medium, and huge, and of course mud to Goose Creek. For clearance, I have the idea of raising the legs of the wheelchair, so Peter's legs stick straight out. I think I'll wrap a rope around a tree to ease him down. Leverage. As I try to tie the rope to his chair, Peter-Andrew is slapping at my hands.

"What, you're picky now? They will never think we would go down there."

"No way am I letting you do this."

"Pfffttt, walk then." I throw the rope at him. "You have control of the wheels."

Team Elmur is hung. We need a miracle. We need legs.

"Hola." Hugo comes down the path.

"Over here," I call. It's Hugo. He's absodefinitely back! He hasn't let us down. The shot of relief, head to toe, makes me woozy. I glance from his face to some plastic bags, and in them are groceries. Man, he comes with legs to spare.

"Que pasa?"

"I'm trying to get this dipwad and his chair down the hill to…to a place to camp."

With the bags on Peter-Andrew's lap, Hugo controls a forward rope that we have looped around a tree and the chair. I am in front of it, as I crest the lip of the trail and begin our descent. Lodge pole pine limbs hang over the path, but not so low that the boughs hit our faces. I break through the long, silver strands of the webs of spiders that hang like crepe paper at a birthday party. A single fly finds the sweat on my neck and refuses to move more than a few inches from my skin at a time, even though I am shaking my head like a maniacal horse. Just twenty feet down, and I already hear the roar of the falls at the creek.

It always interests me that the cell signal is stronger at the bottom of this hill than at my house. I text my grandmother that I am at Andrew's. I text Andrew's mother that he is fine, and is currently Peter Farber, and is filling in the time at my house with my games, and can he spend the night. My Grandma and Andrew's mother have complete faith in each other and won't check. Grandma will be relieved. She will pop open a bottle of beer, take out a frozen dinner, and put her feet up.

Hiding is a skill. It takes food and knowing where to set up camp. We are in a place that no wheelchair could go. That will be helpful. We are close to home though, which is essential for toilet paper. Hugo hiked down Andrew's tent. We think we have some time before the next go round with Stella. I know she is not finished. My diary is too full of possibilities.

Hugo is a boy-scout starting the campfire without clouds of balled up paper. He knows how to campout. I go through the grocery bag. Hugo has brought a large bar of Hershey's chocolate.

"Chocolate!"

Hugo grins back at me. "And marshmallow and graham

crackers and peanut butter. Thought you needed it by now."

"I don't care if the principal sent you."

He looks at me like, *what you say?*

"How'd you think to bring all this?"

"We need carbs, protein and sugar. We need to plan. It could be a long day."

Peter-Andrew is putting marshmallow spread on a graham cracker with the knife Hugo remembered and I am adding the chocolate. Gratefulness, and the fire warm me. I am so grateful and so amazed that Hugo came back with chocolate, came back at all and *with chocolate.*

"I grabbed this for you." He dug into his pocket and then opened his paw. "My uncle makes these to sell on the internet. Thinks he's related to an Aztec chief. He gets them all blessed before he sends them. Sacred thoughts, he says they are.

"I-c-n-o-p-i-l," I read out loud from the stamped leather of the bracelet. "Thanks. I mean really, thanks. Chocolate, food, gifts. It's like Christmas."

He shrugs. "He has a barrel of them. It means, 'worthy of something' in Aztec."

I twirl the bracelet around my index finger. "Worthy of what, you might ask."

"Ok, maybe just 'worthy.' That's enough."

"Why did you want to burn down that sign?" asks Peter-Andrew.

"I hate it."

"You hate a sign?"

"It's the place the sign is in front of. My house was there, the house I was born in. I lived with my parents there, before, when they were still together. The house was ripped from its foundations and moved for those condos. My tree and my swing were cut down. Duke, my first and only dog was dug up."

I shut my mouth. It's all stupid. Everybody has stuff. I hear an animal move in the undergrowth. So what, my parents sold the house and divorced. So what, my father didn't care to push me on my swing anymore; there is no swing anymore.

"So, you want to thank her for flaming the sign."

"From the bottom of my heart."

"Well she definitely has your diary," Hugo says as he flicks embers with a stick. "What else is in it? Anything else she is going to do on your behalf?"

"And blame you," Peter-Andrew adds.

"Only baby-step stuff for Stella. Stuff she can do sleepwalking. Stuff she can do without making it seem weird."

Peter-Andrew snorted.

I stare into the fire. I know that I'm sunk.

"You didn't want to burn anything else down?"

"Burn? No." I pick up a stick and poke at the fire.

"What else?"

I don't want to tell them. I feel the pressure inside that makes me want to be ashamed and guilty, but I can't, not now.

Peter says with his mouth full of peanut butter, "Spit the rest of it out. We need to know."

It's based on the Elements. "Fire…you know. Water, fill Racheal's pink, cool Cabriole. Wind, paint balling Mrs. Seaman's house."

"Mrs. Seaman's?" Hugo asks.

"Elementary school. She used to pick somebody, the first person, to line up for lunch while she shifted stuff on her desk. That person would pick a friend to line up next to her and then that person another friend."

"And you were always last?" Peter knows these things.

"Second to last most times, but I always felt bad for Michael Bolton, the booger man, who was boogerish. Poor guy. He was ALWAYS last." *Shenanigans, absodefinitely all shenanigans.* "If I never return to school, things will be fine."

I stare at my phone expecting it to sing. "I wonder why

I haven't heard from her…you know, gloating?"

"Maybe her phone is still in the box. It's traceable, if you don't want people to find you, disable location services in that thing."

I hold my phone now like its dynamite. As if she heard me, it begins dinging like an exploding doorbell. I'm getting Photoshare notices like a lightening round on a quiz show. Pages of my diary are popping into view. Who I love, who I hate; Stella is snapping pictures of my thoughts by the dozen, all over the world-wide web.

Oh Shitnanigans. I feel as if my guts are being pulled out through my esophagus. It hurt so much, even from Stella. I inhale. The pine smells crisp. I think about that, the crisp smell of the pine. The thing that Andrew and I like is that the outdoors is so not virtual. We come here to detox, to watch the sparks from the fire cremate little holes in things, to eat sand in the food chain. The creek is cold and running fast.

As my phone barks reminders of my fate I say in a defensive outburst, "Some of what is in the diary is funny. I wrote that I was going to put a cow in Mrs. Fielding's classroom." Mrs. Fielding's classroom is on the second floor. "Cows can go upstairs, but they can't come down."

"What about the service elevator?"

"Too small for a cow. I wrote that I was going to release nine chickens into the school numbered one through ten without a number five."

Peter-Andrew's head jerks to look at me. "OMG, that is brilliant."

I don't know why kudos from Peter Farber make me blush. I feel just that little bit better.

"Will she read it all?" I ask as if it's not already been done. "She could get bored of me complaining endlessly." All I know is that people are not kind. A mountain breeze fans my red face.

"You knew that someone was going to be you. Why didn't you put it in a better place?"

"I did! And no one was supposed to go to our homes. I figured there would be supervision. Kaiser said the blend would be hazy."

"You should have put it down the toilet." Peter-Andrew throws his paper plate into the fire.

I watch it burn. Me and fire.

Hugo has moved out of sight. I hear the sound of the snap of a plastic bag being opened. He enters the area of the fire ring. With his adolescent five-o-clock shadow, he is a bear coming into camp. He's not good at growling though. His voice didn't dive too deep. It's weird in such a big guy. I wonder if he has had enough to eat, you know a whole salmon or something. Andrew eats all the time, a constantly grazing Brachiosaurus. Hugo is finishing leftovers before he trashes the cans and paper plates. I've lost my appetite and give him the rest of mine. He eats it in a bite.

"Should we keep an eye peeled for the, you know, the other five elements and try to stop her?" I suggest.

"We need a book of our own," Hugo says as he closes the plastic bag and licks his fingers. "She's got a playbook; we need a playbook. She has shown us her hand. You have never run defense against her, so she will not be expecting it now."

"Yup, she sensed my weaknesses before, and now she knows them."

An irritated Peter or Andrew blurts out. "What have you been afraid of with her? Abject failure, total rejection, persona non grata? Pretty much what you have now. Stand up for yourself! Geez, you beat yourself up more than she does. It's holding you back, Elmur."

"Are we all agreed then?" Hugo is standing at the fire all somber-like, like we are all taking a blood oath. "Stella has snapped the ball. The game is in play. We have surprise on our side. We must not give the initiative to the other team."

I finger the leather wrist cuff that I had slipped on my wrist. I pull at the leather ties. "It's risky."

"Must be real easy for her when you see yourself just

like she sees you." Peter-Andrew is on a roll.

"Shut up Peter. What do you know? You don't know me."

"Ya, sure."

Maybe it's not Peter saying those things. Maybe it's Andrew. Maybe he has wanted to say this to me for a while, and now he can hide behind Peter. Andrew is not Confrontational Man. My palms sweat. In the face of our campfire, I remember the burning sign in front of the condos. Sometimes when something happens that you never thought would, there's a sort of cosmic change, possibilities open. I didn't do it, but it is done. I'm quiet. The creek is tossing head-long over itself in constant sound. It's grinding rocks into sand, but it takes ages and ages. I inhale a shot of invigorating pine. I remember that the sign is dead. Ding Dong, the sign is dead. That stamped board wasn't as potent as I had thought it was. It turns out that I wasn't going to have to look at it forever. Elemental change.

And then I weasel. "They'll rebuild that sign again, and I won't be combined with Spectacular Stella to torch it a second time." I stir my stick in the flames until it begins to burn. In the air, I wave the ember of red at the end of it like it's a wand. Magic, that's what I need. I rub the stick on a log, turning it, sharpening it.

I finally flip the battery out of my phone and pocket it. I'm relieved that I have made it gone quiet. "Pretty much EVERYONE is in the diary," I say as I use my other hand to throw in a pinecone to watch it flare up, fizzle and spit. Peter-Andrew wheels himself to the tent. The Andrew in Peter-Andrew is done, maybe the Peter in Peter-Andrew as well.

Hugo and I are quiet. He doesn't talk of plans, or playbooks. He is finding out that I do give up. I am sitting with my not-magic stick in the sadness of blown expectations again, when I hear a whisper of air movement pass my ear. Whap. Something explodes behind me. Liquid, bright red, runs down the brown trunk of a tree.

Whap, whap, whap, whap, whap. Each sound a different

color. Andrew's tent suddenly looks like a finger painting gone mad. I take a glancing hit off my shoulder and the paint drenches my arm. Hugo dives on top of me, and we both hit the ground hard. Pine needles stab my lips. I follow the big guy in elbow-walking towards a dense strand of trees. I glance at the tent. Peter-Andrew has gone inside.

"What do we do?" I yell at Hugo who, along with me, has his back against a solid trunk. At this point there's enough paint, to open up a store. I quick-glance around the side of the trunk.

"They are going flank us," I yell.

"What?" He yells back, his voice suddenly loud as the shooting ceases.

"At least seven. I saw four, and then three." I glance again. I pull my head back and immediately balls pellet the tree.

"They're repositioning," he says quietly.

"I know."

"Let's set up a screen."

"What?"

"Crawl to a position in a straight line from where they are going to flank us. You go to one side. I'll go to the other. Lay low in the brush. Let them come through us."

"What about Andrew?"

"Doesn't he have stuff in there?"

"He won't walk."

"His shelter is solid. We have to get them to retreat. Whoever comes closest to you, tackle them, trip them up and take their gun. Keep doing it that way. We'll gain some ammo at least."

"I don't do this in real life. The odds—"

"Watch their eyes, watch which way they move and strike at their weak side. If necessary, you gotta wrap up."

"Wrap up?"

"First rule of tackling: wrap your arms around the guy before you put him onto the grass. If you don't grab him it's just a hit. They can slide off a hit. If you have to hit, hit them hard enough that they can't come back on you.

Hugo leaves me, my belly in the wet, cold dirt. I move closer to thick bush. As I wait, my chin on the ground, my mouth blows air in puffs that disturbs the granules of dirt in front of it. I watch for, listen for, shoes breaking twigs in the forest. What I'm really hoping is that they will all "screen" over to Hugo. He could wrap up a dozen or so and throw me one to hold up for the picture at the end.

Geez, I'm thinking, *even if I manage to get a weapon, every person I ever wrote about in my diary could be out there hunting me down.*

I swallow and try to ignore a frantically hard-beating heart. When a deer becomes motionless, its large ears listen, its muscles tense, its nerve endings pop. That's me and my body is pumping full of adrenaline. I need to imagine myself with antlers, long, pointy, hurty things that will pierce my opponent. Deer don't think, they put their heads down and charge.

I hear the crunch of footsteps, careful steps that follow each other slowly. I close my eyes and try to think of myself more as a bear or something that rises onto its haunches and roars and bares teeth and claws. I'm just over five feet tall, but I have a brown belt. I've never fought a person who wants to hurt me though.

I hear the cry-outs of what seems like three people. Hugo must have opened his big eagle-like wings and brought them down on a fly over. The footfalls near me are getting closer. What did the Big Guy say? It's in how they are moving, where their eyes are, if their shoulder dips a little to the left or to the right. That's how to bring them down. So I'm watching. My head is cranked back on my neck and feels like my spine is folded in half. I don't think that I'm blinking.

The first foot I see is a Reebok tennis shoe that I recognize, Holly Thompson, soccer player. I really wanted someone *softer*. Someone less win-at-all-costs. I throw myself around her knees. She screams, a piercing sound, like a machine without oil. "Get off me," she yells. I won't let go, and she goes down badly.

She's stunned when she hits the ground, but she's not "hit" enough. She recovers and punches at my face. The gun she drops is a few feet from us. We grasp at each other, each trying for a wrestling pin that would give us a long enough advantage to reach out for it. Her palm is pushing my head back. Her finger slides up my nose. I can't see the weapon, but I'm reaching for it, getting only air, while trying to trap Holly's arms.

Don't give up.

I don't think Hugo would call this a clean hit. We roll over and over, looking like two octopi fighting. Holly disentangles and flings herself towards the weapon. I try to fling first. I grab the butt of the gun and pull it to my chest. Hugo had said to hold onto the ball. I tuck it under me. I am covering it with my full weight, my elbows in. She is striking my side. I flatten out more over the prize under me.

"Give it up, you stupid thing," she says to me. "You're stupid and you've always been stupid."

My kidneys are being gouged by something pokey. I grunt. I kick back with my leg, bending at the knee.

"You're the stupid thing, toilet wipe," I say into the mud.

She kicks my thigh. As she is retracting her leg for another go, I roll onto my back and shoot. I see her shoulder snap. The impact twirls her sideways. I fire again at her hip. Direct hit. She falls back again.

She throws herself at my eyeballs. I fire again, and she falls back, but she springs forward again like she's been hit from behind. She shakes her hands. Ahhh, nettles. The spines are imbedded in her hands and arms. Sucks.

She glares at me and then runs away into the trees. I aim at her butt, but I don't shoot. Waste of ammo. As I stand and hold her gun at half mast, I stare at her receding body. Feels good to see her run away. Only, until that moment, I didn't know I disliked her that much. Maybe I do dislike everyone. It's like I have to poke a pin into people and then see if they will stay.

The weapon is kind of at my knees hanging off the tips of my fingers. I inhale deeply and sigh the breath out. I notice all the flattened huckleberry bushes around me. *Shenanigans*. That alone can make me cry. It's all just become worse, all of it.

"This way." I hear Holly's voice. She's a competitor. She's coming back, and she's bringing help.

I drop back into the brush. A flutter of panic in my stomach. This is more than paint. I glance around for Hugo. The forest is thick. I hear him and want to get to him. I need to feel him at my back. I have no instructions, and then I feel the paint gun in my hand. I glance at it. I have a weapon with ammo. I raise out of the bushes like a crazy person. This takes them back a step, their eyes wide. I open fire, walking towards them as I shoot. Every shot counts. I am ruthless, because there is too much anger stored in my body, and I feel it in my trigger finger. I smile when my opponents' backs turn purple and orange.

A shot takes my shoulder. I am flanked, and I have to take cover. I am panting. The rough bark of the tree molds a pattern against my back. My head is tipped back. Element of surprise, I'm thinking, element of surprise. I crouch down and then lay down with my legs stretched out behind me. My elbows are on the ground, with the gun in front of me. I can't run from this position. No going back. Listening for foot falls, I steady my breathing. I only have two more shots. Twigs snap behind the tree. At the sound of two cautious steps, I aim up, my sight following the line of the gun, and fire twice. I manage two on the chin. He eats paint and drops his gun. I pick it up while shooting with the other hand.

The blitzkrieg overwhelms him, and he drops to his knees, his hands over his face. Her teammate has fled, and isolated, Holly retreats. They have always worked in packs.

That's how they are strong. Get a popular person alone, and it's a new game, a different person.

Score, I think as I throw the straps of the paint guns over my shoulder. I am a weathered soldier after my first skirmish. I take in the damage. Cuts, blood. My nose is bleeding. I feel the drip of corpuscles run into my mouth. I taste the iron platelets. I put pressure on the bridge of my nose. The weapons bounce on my back as I limp towards the tent. I have unarmed the enemy. I have hung onto the ball. I have deflected their advance. Stood my ground. Peter would say that's an improvement, so at least there is that. "At least," I say, as if it is a small thing. The leather bracelet on my wrist that says, "Icnopil" isn't brown anymore. I have to rub it on my pants to see the word. The leather already appears old and worn beyond its moment in time, but the strap tying it to my wrist has held.

At camp, Hugo stands over a mountain of booty. I throw my two trophies on his pile, and I listen to myself tell Hugo that three people "screened" my way. Scratches on my knees and elbows sting and a big cut across my forearm has beaded up red, and then I notice Peter-Andrew wheeling out of the tent flap. The bit of fabric on his shoulder that rubs against the tent flap is painted.

He turns to his creation, the tent. It means something that he is still staring at it. Still staring.

I walk over. I kneel at the chair and put my hand on his knee. "I'll wash it. I promise." The bright colors are beginning to look set, less gooey-drippy. The red color screams at me; you did this, this is your fault. Maybe the Andrew in Peter-Andrew has stroked out. His is so quiet, and he spent a year, a full year threading, weaving really, the special fabric that carries a charge and is a screen, that is impermeable to water and sun.

The tent looks like a rainbow now. A colored-out-of-the-lines rainbow. An ugly rainbow. We won't be friends anymore. Me and the tent are bleeding red. As I watch Peter-

Andrew with his open mouth and his staring eyes, I feel the cold of the saturated sweatshirt on my back. I feel the glue of the paint making my skin itch. I smell like plastic. At least three people hate me more than ever, and now Andrew.

Peter-Andrew tips his head like he's looking at a painting. "It's less grey."

I can't figure out who is talking. What is happening people? When will it end? How will it end? I'm cold and muddy and painted red. I have no idea what she will think of next.

Chapter Ten

When life gets so confusing that another person is running around being you, and being you probably better than you are you, it is time to back-capture points. Stella is in this to flame me. As if she were standing here, she did this to Andrew's tent. I may not defend myself, but I do my friends. I throw back the flap to Andrew's psychedelic tent and walk straight to some pockets in the back. I take out a carefully wrapped bundle and hold it as if it is the most precious thing ever, because it is.

"It's a mess out there. So much crazy with you around." Peter-Andrew wheels himself inside.

"You know you can walk," I say passing by him.

"My legs are not healed."

"Your brain is not healed."

"Back outside, I have to see Peter's point. It is a mess of paint, trampled plants… the tent. I sit on log and unwrap Andrew's three-dimensional print-out air gun. I open the back, see the pellets, and click it shut. It is locked and loaded.

"It's just an air gun," Peter-Andrew says as he watches me.

"Can you make one from a drawing?" I wrap it up again. "As Hugo says, she's out of control."

"You going all 'make my day,' and going 'lone shooter' on her?"

"Got any good ideas yourself?"

"You know her, Peter. Where do you think she is?" asks Hugo.

Peter-Andrew shrugs. Maybe he has to protect her being one of her friends. How could he even want to do that after what he has seen?

"What about you, Hugo? Any guesses?" I ask.

"She's hiding somewhere."

"Getting others to do her bidding."

"We have one advantage." Interjects Peter-Andrew.

"I don't think I should ask what."

"She thinks you're dumb."

"Get stuffed." Out of this whole stupid experiment, I just wanted to roll acceptance around in my brain, kick the tires. Instead I seem now to be public enemy number one. My name is traveling the circuit. Gran and I are going to have to move. If only. Gran has lived her whole life in her house, since she was a girl. Her neighbors are family. Her house wraps around her like the curlers in her hair. I've run out of safe houses.

I'm cold and a little sore where the paint balls hit. I'll check the bruises out later. My paint-gluey clothing has dried firm. We need to clean up and get safe. If I'm found, Peter-Andrew will be sent home to his own devices, and I will be brain-picked like an alien capture. I don't know where she is. She's not going to allow herself to be caught and tethered to a chair with adults yakking at her. We both need room to maneuver. Team Elmur has only one more place to go that we won't be bothered, Hugo's house.

It's cold in the mountains when the sun goes down in May, but sunset is coming later. "We should break camp and go somewhere to clean up." I look at the Big Guy as I say it. I smile a tentative smirk. I'm so glad he's here. It could be just me and Peter-Andrew, a product of bad science, but it's not. I owe him. Whatever he needs or wants, Hugo just has to ask.

I shove the gun into my waistband. Peter-Andrew is right about its effectiveness, but at least I can shoot someone's eye out. I feel better doing something.

I don't like competition. People who don't like competition never win. It's a mind thing. Like I can't play softball. I can't hit a ball while standing all alone at the plate with everyone watching. When I moved in with Gran, she made me pick a sport to play, any sport. She told me that I needed to learn how to lose and keep going. You'll never, ever win, Laura, if you don't play. To my shock and horror, video games didn't count. I chose swim team. I may lose as an individual, and still win as a team. Only to my surprise, I don't always lose. When I dive into the pool, I zone. I just swim as fast as I can. If I win, it's a surprise. I am not competing, I am swimming, and I like swimming.

As if he can hear my thoughts, Hugo says, "You did great today. You played hard and you played clean."

"Maybe too clean…to win." I tell Gran that it may be important to learn to lose, but once in a while, ya know like every century or so, ya have to have a win to keep hope alive.

"La madre que te pario! You won clean. It is good. Look they are gone. This mess is their fault. They brought the paint-ball guns."

Yup. I'm a winner. I sling a backpack over my shoulder. "Can we go to your house Hugo? Unless you've got another idea?" As we shove the chair up the hill, I glance once back at the tent. It's hard to leave it like this. Maybe I should hose it down or something. I'm afraid to do anything until Andrew is back, but then it will be too late. Maybe, if I'm such a winner, the paint won't interfere with the electrics, and it might become a protective shell for the tent. I hope.

At the top of the hill, Hugo and I shrug why-not at each other when we look at the scooters. Peter-Andrew is getting good at being supercharged. Hugo finds Andrew's mother's bike. When we pass the burned sign again, I nearly twist my head off my neck staring at it. It's still smoking.

Now that is one vicarious win.

The firetrucks are gone. As I glance forward. I am inches from an electrical pole. A glancing blow tips me off balance, and I hit the ground. I roll onto my glutes and rub my shoulder. I brush my hands together to get rid of the grit.

"I'm okay," I yell to Peter-Andrew, but he is driving on. The scooter appears to be okay. I hold my breath waiting for the engine to catch. There's a sort of pressure in the air, like nothing is right and something is going to blow. It's giving me goosebumps. The rest of the team Elmur is tearing down the road. I peel out. In the mountains, stragglers are left to the wolves.

I follow Hugo on back streets. When I meet a main Street, I need cover; they are ahead of me. It's one of those Murphy's Law sort of things. The street is empty; I begin my dash across just as a police cruiser turns the corner. My startled eyeballs lock with the startled eyeballs of the driver. He has a picture in his left hand that he in glancing at as he drives up. I pull my hat down low. I am glad for the paint on my face. I don't turn my face from him but ease it around so he has my profile. He doesn't have his foot on the accelerator. He studies me for three heart stopping minutes. When he drives off, I need to stop for a second to breathe and collect myself.

"How far is your house," I call to Hugo when I catch him in another alley.

He grimaces. "'Bout a mile. Up there."

He points to the top of another hill or really una montaña that overlooks the lake. I know the scooter won't make it with Andrew. I glance at the wheelchair and I think of a movie in which the family startle the young man, who thinks he can't walk but can, into standing. Maybe a bullhorn next to Peter-Andrew's ear, or we could throw him in the lake, or stab his leg with a knife.

I'm thinking of some shock treatment when a choir of sirens erupts into the relative calm of the evening. One siren is an attention getter. Five are chilling. Must be the town's entire fleet.

"Can they arrest me for someone else being me?" I say into the glances at me from both Hugo and Peter-Andrew.

The cars are closing in. We peel out of the alley. "I'll meet you there. Don't let Andrew out of your sight," I yell at Hugo.

I promised, promised Andrew that we would stick together. Best I can do now is let them see me. I choose the narrow, dirt road that seems less traveled...away from Hugo's house. The squeal of a dozen tires is kind of funny. They're all after me, a fourteen-year-old girl...with a brown belt in Karate. My bad self. I push my scooter to its limits. Its parts screech. In a single day, I am breaking everything Andrew has made.

A scooter can't outrun a car. In another second I will be in a cruiser's headlights.

Hugo's voice in my head is sending me into the fray, and talking fast, the words tumbling over each other, like timeout is over and the game is being lost. *In a draw-play the Quarterback brings the ball to the runner. HE MUST CONVINCE THE DEFENSE THAT HE IS DROPPING BACK TO PASS. Look ahead. Know where your receivers are. Be bold. Don't give up on a play.*

"Fake them out," I say as I push the red button on the scooter. "Be unexpected."

I "speed" back down the road from where I came. When they pass me, I hear the tires of the patrol car screech to slow and then turn, very satisfying. I still have the paint gun slung over my shoulder. I am a good shot. Andrew and I practice with his homemade infrared gun. Should I shoot at the police? Not a good idea in any playbook. Maybe just shoot their windshield with orange. Bella Stella's goal must be to get me arrested. She has enough info to shame me forever, but that's not enough. Anaphylactic. She wants to take me down, all the way down to hell.

I take a right onto Lake Access Road. All of the turns off the road are short, unpaved, spider-web networks of roads that end at the lake. A forest of trees line both sides. As the black and whites turn the corner, I duck down a familiar street. Some of the roads along the lake don't have names. When the roads run out, I jump off the scooter and run where they can't go. The cops leave their cars to chase me on foot. Now they are running behind me. They have longer legs than I do, more strength, but more weight and big bellies. One talks into his shoulder walkie-talkie. He's calling for backup. *Perfect,* no idea where to go, and I'm already slowing. I glance back. The cops are sprinting. They are in better shape than I would think.

If they take me in, she has won. I know that. *Why*, I ask myself? *What have I ever done to her, but wanted to be her?* I am only one layer of houses away from the beach, and then only water in front of me and cops behind.

My breath is coming harder now. The stitch in my side is an arching pain. The Law are close enough that I can hear their breathless conversation with each other. I cross another street and dive into the darkness between a house and a condo building. I'm running obstacles now, garbage cans, canoes, weathered water skis and broken paddles

If I'm hauled in, they will fingerprint me. I'll have a record. I will be a JV felon. I hop a fence and stop and lean against it. They are not good climbers. Over-winded, I bend at the waist. I'm going to vomit. I hate that. It's a childhood fear that I'll choke on undigested carrots. It began when Gran made me take horse-sized fish pills when I was nine because she read it would help my grades at school.

Pressing up from the fence, I stagger forward towards the house. As I lean against the corner of the building, the cops' voices on the other side of the fence startle me. It's like they're in my lap. This is the Smith's house. On my side of the fence in her kennel is Genie the German shepherd. I hear the cops jumping, trying to see over the fence. The Smiths have security motion lights all around the back yard. I'm small. I stay flat, like a paper-doll, to try to be invisible. I glance in windows that have their shades drawn to the sun. A cop, who is hoisting his body over the fence, is reflected in the glass. It's not easy with so much stuff attached to his body. He keeps getting stuck.

I catch my breath when, out of anxiety, I move too much and I'm spotted. I run to Genie. She doesn't like boys, men, whatever. She smells a boy and bam, she barks like it's a criminal invasion. I push the bolt. She runs over me to get out.

Strike one for the fake out play.

Gran would be upset to see me in jail. I just don't think that I can convince the police that a girl from school who had my genes injected into her and has my diary is doing the moments-of-anger stuff I wrote down.

With Genie handling the cops at the fence, I dash towards the street. Pfffttt if the other cops aren't waiting. I hear my shoes skid on the loose pack gravel. I'm thinking of climbing a pine tree. They'd never find me there. I head across beaches and over docks toward the Kendal's yard. I used to play with Mickey Kendal until he told me that I was too loud all the time. That's another thing. You can't gene-correct for loud or for tact, or for mean. Mickey Kendal is mean, but he had a great climbing tree.

I'm concentrating on getting to the tree, doing the unexpected, faking them out when, just as I am up on the first limb, a hand grabs my ankle and holds me fast. I hold on too, to the limb, and I kick at his grip.

"Stop moving. Any fool should know that you don't burn down signs."

He hasn't enough leverage to pull me down with my arms wrapped in a choke hold around the tree trunk.

"I didn't do it," I say in my loud, mad voice.

"Sure. You running to keep yourself fit?" he asks.

"Because you will never believe me."

He tugs at my leg and scrapes my arms down the bark. I stare down at his longer than a mile forehead and sun damage spots. Gravity has lengthened his red, unsmiling, bulldog face. The cop's large nose is red and seeping from his exercise. His eyes bulge from exertion and from being seriously annoyed. If I don't get loose from him, if he takes me in, I wonder if she will stop or whether she'll keep going sharing every thought I've ever had one page at a time. With me behind bars, she'll have to stop the criminal stuff.

There is a little voice from a big Hugo in my head that says, break the tackle. I can't think how. I'm small and the cop's hands are like from a steel robot. If you are getting tackled around the stomach, keep your legs moving. Stay up. Get your legs out. My one legs is still free. I kick out again and hit the jackpot. His nose. His shoulders kind of collapse inward, and he lets go of me. I'm almost too surprised to remember to drop onto the ground. I must have broken it. Bad news.

I hear large waves lapping the side of a dock. The lake. I have no idea how it will help me, but it's the only direction left to go. I sprint towards it across the lawn. I have trapped myself, and all these angry men will be coming at me from all directions like red, biting ants.

At the water's edge, I wade in. I can swim faster, faster than the cops with their shoes and stuff, but the lake is still full of snow-melt water. I feel the cold by degrees saturate my shoes and pant legs, raising goose bumps. It has frozen my feet in seconds. I won't get far enough, or even be able to stay in long. I glance from the cops to the lake. The men are the width of the lawn and the beach away. I can almost smell their bad breath.

Sometimes I pray. Sometimes I just so want to believe there is some supernatural force helping me, and I like the idea of angels, invisible kind beings helping me cross the bridge over the angry water. My Hail Mary pass is when my eyes rest on an ancient jet ski with the push-on, black plastic key in the ignition.

The clear water swirls around me as I wade to the dock. The jet ski spent the winter in the ice, too old for anyone to take care of it. With freezing fingers, I pull at the rope to free it from the dock. It has been nautically tied and pulls away after the end loop has been unknotted. I place my foot into the narrow ledge around the saddle of the jet ski. I hop twice trying to get some momentum to straddle the seat over the engine. The jet ski rocks and water sucks against it.

The problem with these old, old jet skis is that they have a two-stroke engine that is unreliable in starting, and this one has been abandoned. *Hail Mary.* I pull off the suction-cup-like key and then put it back. Nothing, no characteristic double beep. Glancing behind me I try again, pressing hard on the cup part. Nothing. The cops are running down the beach length.

Please, please, please, please, please! This time, I jam the key in. Beep, Beep. "Oh thank you, thank you, and thank you."

I press the start button. The engine revs, over and over. It won't catch. I pulse the gasoline toggle. I press the start button. Wrrrr, wrrrr, wrrrr, wrrrr. "Get going ya last hope."

The exhaust is thick, and I'm in a cloud that smells of semi-burned gasoline. The cops are nearing, one step from the dock and then one reach from the dock to the back platform of the jet ski. The engine catches. With the gasoline toggle full in, I roar off. The cop falls forward into his deserved icy bath. It's good for what ails ya. *Ha!* My back spray showers the other cop with icy lake water.

Jubilation! I skim the lake while fist-pumping the air. My jet ski and I glide through the swirling tints at about 35 miles per hour. I'm gone.

In the middle of the lake, I release my sore, aching thumb from the accelerator and let the machine slow and the engine idle. The principal had asked me where I would go. Where would I go if I had suddenly become someone else, someone I thought I rather die first than harbor in my cranium? Where would I go to hide? It suddenly, and finally came to me, it is right there in front of me. I would go to the island. She isn't on the island though. I know that now. She's not like Peter-Andrew. She isn't me. She is herself knowing me. Stella is doing everything I wanted to do, but she is not doing it as me. She is not doing it from where I'd run to. She is somewhere she knows that I would never look.

I call Peter-Andrew. "I'm on a jet ski. Meet me at the canoe rental place. I'm fine. Hurry. I'm really cold. Bring a towel, and a coat and some really warm socks."

I press the accelerator again, and I lean forward as the jet ski leaps forward. My fingers and legs are numb from the water splashing on them. I wish I had Andrew's thermal dry suit. In it he looks like one of those long balloons that clowns twist into dogs and hats and stuff, but he is warm and dry. Andrew doesn't like to be cold and wet.

I ride the lake, hiding in the shadows of the pines along its edge. The patrol boat will be on the water soon. They'll have to put it in first and put in a charged battery. That will take time. I need to give Hugo time to get Peter-Andrew and the scooters to the meeting place.

After about twenty minutes on the water, my body needs thawing out. The lake is spring-melt calm, and I glide through the dark water easily. I smell the pitch of the pines. A bat swoops close to my head. I hear the grinding of a boat motor. My head whips around. The patrol boat has a flood light on the water. I realize that I didn't disable location services in my phone.

You are so stupid. Stupid, Stupid, Stupid.

I spy Hugo, the chair, and Peter-Andrew coming down the slight hill from the road. I have to drive the jet-ski away from them. I don't want the police to know Andrew and Hugo are helping me.

The gray boat accelerates and is soon bouncing over my small wake. I need to go where a boat can't navigate. I speed towards the river that feeds into the lake. I can abandon the jet ski up stream and hide in the trees. I cut the turn towards it. Too much, I flip the jet ski. Water surrounds my body in what feels like pure ice. I kick to the surface and blink water from my eyes.

Nooooooo. She can't win. The engine is running. I push on the side of the jet ski. I will flip it over. The water is too deep, I have nothing to push against with my feet to give me leverage. The jet ski rolls back against me, hitting my head and forcing me under. I surface again. The ski has turned and is blowing air and water into my face. I am blind as the bat I saw on the lake, someone grips me, and I am dragged up. My arm catches on something and skin and muscle rip open. In the boat, I am planted between two big guys. They wrap my shivering body in a blanket. Underneath the cloth, I feel the boat power up. I listen to my teeth chatter. They have me.

Chapter Eleven

I hate spiders. Video games always have them. The nasty things are always getting me. That's why when I game, I always stock up on antidotes. The cops are spiders, and I don't have any antidotes left. No triumphant music for me. The jet ski is turned, belly up and being towed. My arm is gashed to the bone. I am pressed in on either side, and I am without Andrew.

At the city dock, the cops move me to a cruiser. Cop number one opens a medic box and grabs cotton and a wrap. He presses the cotton into the wound, and I scream. He ignores me and wraps it with a self-securing arm bandage. Cop two discusses with cop one about stitches. He angles his head and talks into the remote at his shoulder. "Keep your arm up," he says to me. "To stop the bleeding."

I need to let Hugo and Peter-Andrew know that I'm not going into lockup just yet. Can't think of a way. My phone is wet. I'm mummified in a dense blanket, in a cop car with locked doors. I search the street for the Big Guy. I mean, it could happen.

The sirens are the best part of my day. The sound is loud in the car, and I wonder if police ever go deaf. As I watch cars move out of our mow-em-down way, I'm sorry that the hospital is now only about ten blocks away. Next, I am unwrapped, and then a couple of nurses, with cold hands under my armpits, lift me to a gurney.

The hospital is like an airport at Christmas. I see Holly walking out with tape on her nose. Her face is like an over-inflated pink balloon. I find that even though there is a gigantic amount of people in line, cops don't have to wait. I am grateful for the indoor heating. I wonder if the doctors will also be treating me for frostbite.

Cops One and Two were rough handlers, like a gorilla tossing around a bad banana. The hospital staff is better. Still, my arm is throbbing. My body shudders as the warmth works through me. The nurse holds my arm and the doctor is squeezing a few drops of fluid out of a syringe before injecting the juice into my skin. I call the fury of the Gods on Stella Constance Miller's head. I call out for my Gran.

"We'll call her," says the nurse.

Gran hates hospitals.

Poked, stitched, and an hour later I am wheeled out through the white double doors to wait under guard. The first person I see is Principal Kaiser. *Shenanigans.* The day is just getting better and better. He glares at me. *Very professional.*

"The problem is," I say to the principal's back as he walks down a hallway, "she has my every waking thought, but I have none of hers. My life from the first bell of school to the last has always proven that I have no idea how she thinks. She's the demon to my nightmare."

The principal didn't hear anything, and he isn't listening anyway. Nobody listens. We should be exchanging ears not genes.

The gorillas wheel me to a seating area. I'm a minor, and the hospital needs Gran. My white bandaged arm looks like I've been spliced with a snowman. The chair rolls without a bump on the linoleum. I notice that my shoe is still missing, and I wonder if they are going to fingerprint me while in a hospital gown, because I'm still in it and my wet clothes are a ball under the gorilla's arm. As the wheels of the chair roll, a thought begins in my head.

You can walk. You can walk. You can run. A dash for my life here in this place would be unexpected. What else is unexpected is an elevator not five steps from me that has just emptied… and nobody is going up. While cop one signs me out, I moan and then gag like I'm going to explode. Cop two takes his eyes off the ball to signal a nurse. The one thing I do know about sports, never take your eye off the ball. I am out of the chair and aiming to hit the hole between the doors of the closing elevator. A door bangs my cut as I slip though. Pain jabs my body. I'm shaking. As I'm about to punch a floor number, I remember that if you hit the close door button and a floor button at the same time, the elevator will not stop. It's like a direct flight. I hear the cop banging on door. Like that is going to help him. I push "close" and third floor. It's not much. I wish I could do floor thirteen, but it's all I got. Ding, the door opens, and I sprint for the empty nurses' station.

It's lunch time. All the personnel are delivering trays. I can't stay here long though. I keep watch—my head an observant orb behind an as-of-yet-undelivered spray of roses and stargazer lilies. A cop gets off. The flowers are making me want to sneeze. I squeeze my mouth shut and plug my nose. This cop is a new one. The gorillas have called in reinforcements. My play was to get back on the elevator, but I can see that needs adapting. As the blue uniform goes around the corner, I edge down a hallway in the opposite direction.

He has circled back. I am spotted, but I'm close to my target. I used to volunteer here. I know the place. I tug open the door to the laundry chute. It's not a vertical drop. I'm going to have to stuff myself in feet first. I still can't feel a thing in my dead arm as I drag a chair to the wall. I stand on it and put in one foot in the tube and then the other. I sit on the lip of the sill. One cop is so close his sweated brow is splashing me. He has run the length of the hall. With an imp of a smile, I shift my butt muscles and begin my slide. I push my upper body around to fit through. I cop grabs my hair just as my full body enters the chute and beings to slide to the basement. He tears out a handful. *Useful DNA,* he's probably thinking.

In sliding two stories to the basement within a metal sausage wrapper, I burn my hospital-gown-exposed butt. A jagged edge of metal tears a gash across my knee. Turdis Maximus all of it! I wonder if Hugo will be able to push two wheelchairs.

I hobble around working through the pain. Never give up on the play. The cop who only managed to get my hair in his grasp will call in another cop or two in a wink of my eye. Where does that chute go to, I image them asking. They are running here as I limp to the door of the room laundry. I try to think of where to go next.

If I ever get my hands on that girl, I will be as gentle as the cops have been to me. I edge open the door. I hear male voices. Could be any males, hospital staff, but I still can't go that way. I lock the door and pace the room. The doorknob turns, then shakes. A nervous fusion passes through my body. I nearly twist my head off my neck searching for some exit. There's a basement window. Great! I'm small. I rush over to climb onto the table underneath the window. I hit some soap or floor wax or something cleaning related and my bad leg slides. I hit the floor with the only part of me still without a bruise, my head. *I will sue.*

I think I must have knocked myself out, because as my eyes focus again, I note that I'm lying down. The gorilla is still pounding on the door with his big gorilla fists.

"Stand out of the way of the door," he calls.

"Ohhh pfffttt." I sit up while holding my head. I move now as if I'm underwater. I hoist myself onto the table using a chair to step up on. The window is stuck tight. *Shenanigans.*

Deception, Hugo's voice is in my hurt head. I try to think through the pounding of heart and head. The first thrust against the door. It holds. There is nothing in this room but washers, dryers, and this one lonely window that will not open under my feeble strength. If it would only open. I pull again. Another heavy thud on the door. The lock begins to split. I pull the window and rattle its sash. The glass cracks. I use my snowman-like arm to increase the break. I grab a pink, plastic bottle of laundry soap to break shards of glass until the window is glass free.

Another bang on the door. It will break under the next blow. Not enough time to skinny out. I grab the back of the chair I had stepped up on and lift it onto the table to look like I used it to hoist myself through the window. I jab the tip of my finger with a piece of glass and hold the sill of the window until the blood soaks the wood. I jump off the table and onto the floor. A half second before the final blow, I dive into a pile of bloody, life and death infected sheets. I arrange the pile over my head and body and huddle there as the lock gives. The only thing I am thinking as I listen to the bass voices in the room, and around the window, is I hope I don't get sick from the smell, or some disease.

The window-ruse works. The cops dash back out the ruined door. I breathe easier. My head drops against the not-white bedding.

Still, they are all over the hospital.

I'd try to fit through the window, but that's where they will be next, and I'm in a hospital gown. I am naked from the back down. *Geez-Louise*. An idea bubbles up and tickles my liver. Diversion, deception. I have to get back upstairs.

I find a vacant wheelchair and sit into it. I push close to the elevator, where once an elevator arrives, and I see it's empty, I can push on in. Back on the second floor, where they will no longer be looking for me, is the empty nurses' station. Why is there never a nurse at the nurses' station? Not sure about the rest of the poor sods in here, but it's good for me. I roll down to the first patient's room. Two sick souls in there, I move on until I find a room with one person in a two-man unit.

I close the curtain around the empty bed and put the tray table where the people in charge can see it so they know that there is no food tray to pick up. Game, according to Gran, is planning the next move and then the next until you either win or lose.

Orange and red colors from the flashing lights of the cop cars in the parking lot revolved around the room like a roaming sunset. I won't be able to look to Hugo to get me out of this. And anyway, they might be caught. They might have bailed anyway. I hope he's taking care of Peter-Andrew.

The person in the other bed is out and softly snoring. What plan am I on now, "A," "B," "C," "D?" I tiptoe to the patient's chart. Mrs. Keller. I glance at her in the bed. She looks like she has rigor mortis. Suddenly, I feel really guilty that I plan to take her clothes. Maybe coming here, she wore her good-luck shirt that her granddaughter gave her, and she wore it to the hospital for that reason, to wear it home when she got better. I can hear nurses coming down the corridor. I don't know if they are coming here. The woman seems peaceful enough. Next thing I know, her heart monitor goes off like a blinking beacon. Mrs. Keller and I may both be dead. I know that MY heart has stopped.

Chapter Twelve

I nearly jump out of my hospital gown at the alarm from the machine Mrs. Keller is hooked to. It's not good, and people will be coming. I flip around like a fish trying to find water. I dive into her closet. All that comes to my mind is what my football-loving gran likes to say to me, a good defense is a good offense. Gran and Hugo would like each other.

Mrs. Keller, or her daughter or someone has hung up the old woman's clothes with the care that assumed Mrs. Keller would need them again. I'm tiny, but solid, and these closets are really small. I step in and close the door. I step out. It's like a coffin-closet. I have to risk the bathroom. At least Mrs. Keller's elastic waistband will make putting her pants on easier and faster. She has underwear that I could take a dump in, and there'd be carry-all room. In my hurry, and for lots of other reasons, I forgo them. The shirt has lots of sequins. If your skin don't shine, wear sequins. *Hurry, hurry, hurry.* The woman is tall. I have to roll from the waistband and the cuff to get the pants to fit. Looking good girl. She has tennis shoes too. Bless you Mrs. Keller. I wish I could borrow her hair too. Gray hair would be a good disguise. I feel that if

Mrs. Keller knew of my dilemma, she would tell me to take her clothes. *Thanks Mrs. Keller. Get Well.*

With a whole lot of nervousness that I have to keep from my face, I walk out of the bathroom, and out of the room wearing the stolen clothes. A nurse rushes by. *Rushes by.* Best screenplay ever.

"Ball is on the move," I whisper to myself as I stroll to the elevators. I practically whistle with my hands in her pockets. I pull out of her deep pockets wads of Kleenex that I hope are unused, and then something solid. It is her cell phone. My prayers have been answered.

It is hard to imagine that only this morning we had all been sitting on the bleachers, all of us whole, all of us in our carefully orchestrated worlds. Jane, beside me, had been popping the gum she wasn't supposed to have and had been listening to music. Andrew had been playing with the snaps on his jacket. Amy had been half asleep with her head on her boyfriend Mike's shoulder. Now, Andrew is confined to a wheelchair and had to watch as his precious tent was being splattered with paint. God, who knows what else for all the others. Well-meaning people are the worst. Dodge them all like there is no tomorrow.

My head is down, but there isn't much action going on. Everyone is eating. The nurses are at their station, finally, gossiping. *Ding.* The elevator doors slide open.

There are people on deck. Perfect camouflage. This is why I didn't take the stairs, too isolated.

The elevator bounces to a stop and the doors open again. I stay behind a large woman, like she is my mother. People think I'm way younger than I am, and the sequins help. Sequins are for the very young and the incredibly old.

The hospital floors gleam white, the walls are white with a grey strip of wood the length of the space. There are some nurses' carts with computers on top. I am strolling as if I haven't a care in the world, until I see cops at the automatic-open front doors. I slip through the opening of an unlocked door, a storage room. Time Out.

I am in a forest of silver IV poles. It reminds me of a medieval weapons locker. I pick one up. It's light, but the base is awkward. I tuck it under my good arm. I feel its weight, and find its balance, and breathe a few deep breaths. I'm going to have to ignore my ankle and my arm. It will take full body motion to go all Friar Tuck with this pole. I peek out the door. Yup the cops are there. I don't feel really confident. Two of them, one of me. They are stronger, able to take this weapon off me in a second. All I have to do is surprise them and get out the door. *Get out the door*.

As I am trying to psych myself, I hear singing and horns blasts. Down the hall, in the depths of the hospital, there seems to be a Mexican fiesta going on.

La cucaracha
La cucaracha
Ya no puede caminar…

Cinco de Mayo. Today is May fifth? It is May fifth. The children's ward piñata party is winding down. Like I said, I'm real young looking for my age. I'm bandaged up to my armpit. I'm a chameleon in a children's ward. I'm relieved when I get to put down the IV pole. I'll just wheel it down to the party beside me. I hang a bag from it. Blend in baby.

The piñata bursts and candy rains. There's a balloon clown. I ask for a balloon hat, that I pull way down on my head. When I see a family of five putting their kid into a bed in the big room of beds and saying goodbye, I edge my way over to them. As I go, I grab a coat and struggle into it.

Red balloon hat on head? Or coat hood on head? Coat hood, balloon hat in hand.

As the fantastic-five family leaves the ward and walks to the exit, I stay close by them. I hope my proximity makes me seem like I'm one of them. They are my blockers, the great fake.

When the outside air hits my face, I'm so relieved that I want to close my eyes to it, but I'm only just out there when a cop says, "Hey young lady."

"Turdis Maximus."

The cop calls again, "Stop."

If I stop, I'm sunk. If I don't, I'm sunk. I hear his shoes on the pavement closing in. I plow through the family of five. It's no use. He'll collar me with his long cop's arm. *So close.* All that diversion for naught.

Next thing I know Peter-Andrew is careening down a ramp in his wheelchair. Pushing on his wheels, he aims himself towards the knees of the cop. I am walking fast, then faster. Peter-Andrew takes the guy out like a bowling ball and a pin. What a great tackle by a disabled crazy person. My rescuer throws himself from the chair and is moaning on the ground. Hugo grabs my arm, and we go the other way.

As we turn the corner of the hospital, I toss the balloon hat. In the parking lot, he stuffs me under an SUV.

"Wait!"

I watch his shoes leave me. I lay for a long time, long enough that my neck is beginning to hurt from holding my head up. When I rest it, gravel cuts into my cheek. *Forget it.* I begin my wiggle out from under the car, and I see shoes, *ah come on!*

Hang on—Hugo's tennis shoes.

"Come on," Hugo says as he leans over to look at me under the car.

"What took so long?"

"I wanted to make sure they were off your track."

I crawl out.

I turn and hug Hugo. He hugs me back.

"Good work," we both say together.

"How did you know where to find me?"

"The city's whole squad of cars is sitting outside the hospital."

"Where have they gone?"

"Stella has been busy."

I have never felt so cold. No more post-winning game glow. Stupid diary.

Like he read my thought, Hugo says, "In fairness, who could have guessed something like this?"

"In fairness," says I, "who, with something like this coming, and with my Gran as a prognosticator, wouldn't have burned that book into a thimble of ashes?"

"Luck didn't play you fair."

"When does it ever. Whatever. I do have some good news; I have a phone I can't be traced to." I pull it from my pocket.

~

We meet Peter-Andrew at hole number one of the Frisbee golf course across the street from the elementary school.

"Don't go over there, but I just pushed past the front of the middle school. Did you write something about painting the school in your tell-all book? I'm just spit-balling here, but I take it from the way your eyes are googling out that that is a yes."

"Does it say, death to all tyrants and stupid-faced teachers?"

Peter-Andrew shakes his head like I'm the stupidest. He turns and wheels away.

"I had a good reason," I yell at him. I can feel him, or both of them, rolling their eyes.

Taking turns pushing the hell-chair on the way up to Hugo's uncle's house (can someone not live at the top of a steep hill), I figure that Peter-Andrew must be fake-helping propel the chair forward, and if he isn't, he wishes he'd have thought of it. The house is a chocolate-brown cabin near Bear Basin. I do think of a chocolate house. It's so small it doesn't seem like a whole person could fit into it. It's a little house in the big woods. Hugo's uncle has a few neighbors like hermits and witches. The surrounding is forest. The cops won't find us here.

"How'd you get out anyway?" Peter asks as he rolls up behind me.

"I slid down the laundry shoot and then broke a window in the laundry room for diversion and hid in the pile of dirty laundry.

"That's disgusting. Brilliant, but disgusting. How did you get out of the laundry room?"

"In the children's ward, it was the Cinco de Mayo…balloons…clowns. I blended with a family as they were leaving. I got clothes from the closet of an old lady who I think may have just died."

I am not used to people looking at me with sort-of admiration. Especially people like Peter Farber. I always thought I'd die of shock if someone praised me. I'm not dead. It did make me squirmy though.

"While I was sitting at the top of the ramp, I over-heard that there's a meeting at the school," says Peter-Andrew.

"Principal Kaiser was at the hospital," I say.

"Maybe you should heads-up your gran and Andrew's mom so they know that you're still fine. Don't want them to call the cops on you."

My turn to roll my eyes. Still, good thought.

Large windows that frame forest and sky make the room seems larger, spacious. I look around what appears to be the bracelet-making corner of the room, Uncle's etched silver plates with sayings of valor that he puts on leather strips. There is a leather sewing machine and material in three colors. I pick-up one that says 'Tlamatine.' Another one says 'Oppa ícuitl quicua.' I open the brochure. "'Oppa ícuitl quicura' means double-poo eater."

"What you say?" Peter-Andrew's head swivels toward me.

"You can't have your cake and eat it. Ya can't have it all. They're all Aztec sayings written by Aztec poets. That one 'Tlamatine' means 'the one who knows.' It's the Aztec word for poet," says Hugo.

Seeing the possibilities of "double-poo eater," I scan the brochure. Áiac xictli tlaltícpac... "No one is a belly-button?"

"Everyone has value. Never underestimate people."

"And these are Aztec? The people who had human sacrifices, you know like, by the thousands?"

"They respected people who died honorable deaths over people who played it safe."

"Anyone who has a quote that uses the word belly-button, is good in my books," says Peter-Andrew.

"Why didn't they like navels?"

"Not navels. The word Mexico comes from "metztli," moon, and "xictli" navel. People of the navel of the moon. So that quote is navel of the earth, no one is the navel of the earth."

"I like the one you gave me best."

"Me too. I'm hungry." Hugo opens the refrigerator door. He takes out dough in a bag, a bowl, and then a griddle. The bowl goes in the microwave. He gets out cinnamon and sugar. The griddle heats with no smoke, he rolls out rounds of the dough and tosses each onto the heat. They puff and brown in minutes. From the hot bowl he spreads cooked apples, and then he dusts it all with the sugar and cinnamon and rolls them up. The smell is like Christmas. It's always like Christmas with Hugo. I remove a chair from the table and wheel Peter-Andrew into its slot. I hand him a plate. Thank God Peter had only lost the use of his legs is all I can say.

Hugo is making more, when a car stops in front of the house.

"Your uncle?"

"No."

I bolt out of my kitchen chair and spill my milk on the carpet underneath the table.

Who puts carpet under a kitchen table?!

"For the love of…you have all the finesse of a bull in a china shop," says Peter-Andrew.

"Forget it. Hide," calls Hugo.

There is a pounding on the door. I wheel Peter-Andrew into the only other room in the house. They, whoever they are, won't have to look long.

"Get in the closet," Peter-Andrew says.

"There isn't a closet."

I hear indistinct words at the door. No scuffling, no, "where is she," but footfalls inside the house. In case Hugo has been chloroformed, I head towards the door.

"Come out."

"Is that Hugo?" I whisper to Peter-Andrew.

The bedroom door opens.

Hugo shrugs his shoulders. "It was my uncle's friend. They are getting people together to look for Stella. He wanted uncle's dog. Boozer can track anything. He said the school was a nut house. Parents in the assistant principal's face. Other parents telling those parents to calm down that this was meant to be a great and meaningful thing. Lots of yelling."

"Stella's mother was there. So nobody's found her."

"Your grandmother must have the cops at her door," says Peter-Andrew.

I lean back on the pillows on the bed and close my eyes. I haven't been too kind to my arm and the painkiller is mostly gone. It stings like a hundred yellow jackets have ravaged it. "She's probably heard from the hospital too." I could sleep, I really could.

"How are we going to find Miss Stella?" I ask into the air. It's like its half time, we're down by like fifty, and we have an injured player. "What's she doing right now?"

"You were good dreaming up possibilities for her and writing them down like a playbook."

"Stuff it, Peter."

"No really. She doesn't have that much imagination on her own."

"Whatever."

"She's a one trick pony."

"She was smart enough to sack my room." I finger my bracelet. "Maybe it's time we sacked hers."

"How?" asks Peter.

I glance at the wheelchair. "I have no idea. You?"

Chapter Thirteen

I sat up straighter on the uncle's bed and pushed to the edge. No use getting comfortable. "We need clues. We need to go to her house."

"Maybe she has posted something?"

"And leave an electronic footprint?"

"She not thinking right," says Hugo. "Mira, she is the one doing the things. She could get caught. What is she gonna say? The diary made me do it."

Andrew's phone jingles with a message

There once was a girl who's a dope…

"Here we go."

She has been notified of the demise of my phone by the fact it no longer connects.

I grab the phone from Peter-Andrew, who is now looking over my arm at the phone's screen.

"There once was a girl who's a dope, who's given to a constant mope, she's no longer passive, but right now quite active, while walking a skinny tightrope."

Another message beeps. We are in real time with each other.

Ding dong, the chapel bell, donuts on the table, coffee's in the well.

"She's at Pancakes and Eggs."

"What? How do you know that?" Peter-Andrew grabs the phone back.

I let him have the phone. "It's Monday."

Peter-Andrew is making these duh faces at me.

I have a dream that I'm swimming in a pool and the water is hard, and I have to punch my hand into it and pull back as hard as I can to move forward. Hugo would say that to win, you have to stay positive.

"Father Fudge, ding dong, the chapel bell, he works at Pancakes and Eggs on Saturdays, Sundays, and Mondays." I sigh. "Andrew and I go there, like around eleven on Saturdays for coffee. Father Fudge is Steven Frank. He is a junior. We call him Father Fudge because he is not particularly good at, you know, bringing stuff, like even just coffee and a giant cinnamon roll. Amanda Wright works with him. He has a giant crush on her, and she treats him like her slave. He is so nice, and he tries so hard."

"You were going to do something to him in your diary?

"No. I guess we weren't nice calling him Father Fudge though. Anyway, to Amanda—real blonde hair, blue eyes, big boobs, she'll graduate to working in a bar as a gold-digger when she is old enough. He does all her work and forgets his own. He's gonna get fired. Once, Andrew and I watched as she poured a glass of water over his head and laughed the whole time. I wanted to sock her, but he would have defended her."

"Maybe we should call the cops and tip them off. Let them do the work." Peter-Andrew says. "What did you write?"

"She teases Father Fudge, really mean stuff. It's hard to watch."

"What did you write?" Asks Peter-Andrew again.

"You know, it doesn't matter," says Hugo. "Uncle has two box cars that we made together. They'll get us down off the hill and into town."

"Brakes?" I ask.

"I was going to say engines, but I'll go with brakes," says Peter-Andrew.

"No engine, or brakes. Use your feet."

"Can you steer it?"

"Oh yeah. Good steering."

The one good thing about these cars is that they were made big enough for a Hugo. The Big Guy pushes them out to the end of the driveway. He puts Peter-Andrew in one.

"I'll drive," I say.

"Not on your life. I'll be driving," says Peter-Andrew.

"But you haven't got usable legs."

"I've got arms."

"But no legs. It could be dangerous."

"Your driving is dangerous."

"I've been driving Gran to the doctor and to the grocery store since she lost her driver's license last year. I happen to know that Andrew has never driven. What about you Peter?"

"Every day since I was six."

Probably partially true. We are wasting time. I wiggle in behind Peter-Andrew, my legs around his hips and down along his legs. It is a gravel road for the entire three miles to the paved city limits.

"When we need to brake, I'll just throw you out to work as a drag," the ever-gracious Peter-Andrew says to me.

Maybe it would be better to do this with my eyes shut. Hugo eased the vehicle out to the incline. I decide that braking blind would be no good. I review the look of the journey in my head, bends in the road, and drop-offs on the side, with pine trees— hit a tree trunk and the only thing that gives is your head.

"Got any helmets, Hugo?"

"Por supuesto."

That's better, I think as I put mine on. *Now I can only break my neck.*

Peter manages the first two turns at normal speed. We

have incline but there are some flat areas where I press the plastic bottoms of my shoes into the dirt. I feel the heat of friction through my shoes and to my heels. I nearly break off my foot in a pothole. *Just getting healthier and healthier.*

We skid around bend four. We are moving sideways in the turn. There are no road guards at the edge.

"Ahh, ahh, ahh, ahh..." My shrieking vibrates as we hit washboard.

Peter is throwing the wheel around. On some straight road, I take a second to glance behind and see the canal in the road my feet have dug.

At the bottom, where the back road hits the main road, we blast through the intersection. A car's tires screech. The vehicle turns to avoid the box and the two bobbing heads in it. The car showers us with pebbles as we careen across the road. The back end of the car hits the cart. I think that I'm screaming as Peter-Andrew and I are pushed sideways. I shove my feet hard against the ground. My knees feel the pressure, but I keep my feet down. We hit the brush. It lashes Peter-Andrew's face. Just before we have a head-on with the lodge pole pine in front of us, the box tips up on its nose, and we drop into a ditch.

"Oof," I hear from him as my body is thrown forward and crushes Peter-Andrew against the steering wheel. He is making further pitiful sounds. I smell pine from broken branches. There is dust-grit in my face. I'm chewing on it. It sounds crunchy in my ears.

The guy in the car runs to us. He helps me out. "What the hell? Are you maniacs? God is anyone hurt?"

When Peter-Andrew doesn't get out of the box, the man gets really concerned.

"He's not hurt," I say. "I think. His, his...his legs are repairing and, um…look we are trying to get to his mom at Pancake and Eggs." That didn't make sense. I pressed on. "She forgot his medications and, um, with this experiment at the high school. It's really important that we get to his mom." I finish. I think I am sweating. I'm hot and cold.

Hugo arrives with excellent control. He pushes out of his machine. "We're sorry mister. We are trying to get to the restaurant. It's really important, or we wouldn't have done, you know, *this*." His arm waves globally to the box cars.

The guy is suspicious. "Why didn't you call there?"

"We couldn't," I inject. "We don't have phones with us. Could you please give us a ride? It's only another couple of miles. He needs his wheelchair—"

"I thought you said medication."

"Both, for his legs. Pain, the pain is vicious."

When Hugo lifts Peter-Andrew out of the box, the guy says, "Maybe I should take you to the hospital?"

"Maybe we should let his mom do that?" I suggest.

That hits home. The guy would like to get rid of the three loonies.

~

At the restaurant, we press our noses against one of the windows next to the front door and look in. Between rushes, the restaurant isn't busy yet. The building is rustic, and barn-like with, cherry stain on wide boards. The ceiling is a trestle of beams that hold up the slanted roof. The décor is old timey, like it's from a 1902 edition of The Sears and Roebuck Catalogue. Stuff like, highly polished, quarter sawed oak tables. Sideboards with serpentine shaped tops, blue enamel-ware pots, jars of preserves and beans. Antique boxes of soap powder.

"Let's put Peter-Andrew in this chair. He can trip her as she runs out."

"I see Stella. She and Amanda have their heads close together," Hugo comments.

She really does have great hair," says Peter-Andrew. "I can see why you are jealous."

"Shut your gob, Peter."

"Hey, I'm just saying that you were right. So, what's the game plan, Coach?"

I see Father Fudge hovering next to them picking his eyebrow. It's what he does when he's agitated. They are more than he can handle. With both of them, his head must be close to exploding.

"What were you going to do to her?" asks Hugo.

"Pour a cup of black hair dye over her head."

Peter-Andrew snorts. "Funny, but is that all? We are here to stop *that?* We should have thought this through."

"The point is we have found Stella," says Hugo. "Let's leave Peter-Andrew outside the front door. You sweep right and make sure she doesn't get to a back door. I'll go straight up the middle."

"Our objective here is to get her and drag her to the authorities who are looking for her. I was told to find her, and wa-la, I have. Tackle her, Hugo. I'll be back up."

Peter-Andrew prepares himself in a rustic log Adirondack chair that has a tipped back seat. He complains that he can't use his legs to trip anyone because it might damage them.

"As opposed to all the other things we've been doing? Get creative. I know you can," I say in a fake, bright, encouraging voice.

I go in through the back door, through the Christmas shop at the back of the restaurant. Glittery things catch the falling light that is hitting them through west facing windows. It smells spicy from loads of candles for sale. Stella is at a table towards the back of the restaurant, at a freestanding table instead of a booth.

A person pays his bill at the hostess' station. Now it's only Stella, Amanda and Father Fudge in the place. We don't call him Father Fudge to his face. We wouldn't. It's just that he is so pale under his dark, perfectly combed hair. His mouth is sweetly pink-tinged, his eyes are soft. Zippo self-esteem. He is bait for everyone.

Stella is putting on her jacket and chatting with enthusiasm. Her back is to me. I watch her reach back with her arm to thread it into her sleeve. In seeing her, and after the events of the day, I lose my head and close in too fast, too obvious. I just want to grab that arm and twist. *Ask me now where she is, Mr. Kaiser.*

Almost like her body is in slow-motion time, I watch her turn her head. Her expression turns from happiness to real joy. If I had better genes, I could read that face. If I had better genes, I would have read that face. Instead, I'm too fast off the line. She sidesteps me, and I fall into Father Fudge. I have blown the play. Hugo has good footwork and changes course. If I hadn't gone right for her, Hugo would have her by now.

Father Fudge is up on his feet. He's in a wrestler pose and is glaring at me. I can see in his eyeballs that he knows about "Father Fudge." These are the mistakes I make. These are not the mistakes Stella makes.

He lunges. I move out of his way. He runs into a table and falls in front of Hugo, along with the table, the glasses, plates, and silverware. Father Fudge has taken the big guy down. Bracing himself to get up, Father Fudge puts his hand down on broken glass.

Amanda and Stella circle me. With a single fluid motion, Amanda throws a cup of liquid on my head. Mostly blind now as it runs into my eyes, stinging them, I run into a recovering Hugo. As we both go for the now-exiting-the-building play option, we half run, half stumble to the front door. I fall like a stone across Peter-Andrew's pole that he has substituted for his legs. Everything goes black. More brain damage.

Chapter Fourteen

I didn't read her face. If I had, that brilliant, welcoming smile, the joy there…we, team Murphy, would be looking prettier. She lured me there. My hair is graying, literally from the hair dye they threw on me. My own plan for Amanda, that's rich. On the heels of the most embarrassing moment in any contest between teams, Steely Stella and her first draft players have come out on top. Team Elmur is once more talking about what went wrong. The trouble is we overplayed the down; we overestimated her goals; we overshot her intentions. Even while absorbing our loss, we have to get ready for the next play.

We are on our way to Stella's house. If her mother is looking for her, then she is not doing all this from her home. It's not her headquarters. Don't know how we will get in. We are desperate though. We will find something.

I need to change clothes. Covered in dye, I'm afraid to sit on anything. We check my house first, but it's like jailhouse rock there. The boys in blue are nothing else but persistent. Hugo says he has a little money and on Fridays the hospital thrift shop by the post office is open until eight. He buys me pants and a shirt for less than ten dollars. Sweet, black sweatshirt and pants. It's nice to leave the old lady pants behind.

The Lakeview Lodge is only about a half mile from Stella's house, and they have a canoe left on the beach. The pedestrian gate is open. They don't bother to close it at seven when it's not beach weather. We can approach Stella's from the rear, from the lake.

"There are lots of lake-view windows at the Lodge."

"It's not a busy time for the hotel. Too much mud, lake's barely melted."

We scout the canoe. No one bothers us, and then we find out why. "I can't find any paddles."

We push the wheelchair farther down the lakeside sidewalk until we reach the end and some rockers around a cold, unlit fire pit.

"Now what?" I rock and stare at the lake. "We can't get there by the road."

"We need anything sort of long and flat."

"One of those pool skimmer things on a pole?" Peter-Andrew asks. He is facing us with his back to the water.

Hugo and I turn and look behind us at the hotel's pool.

"Might as well scope it out." Hugo leaves and comes back with swimming pool kick boards.

"Seriously?" I ask.

"Como no? Anyway, the pool shed isn't locked and this is all they have."

I take my shoes off and throw them into the boat. I walk it through the water, back to Hugo and Peter-Andrew. I'm thinking of dunking my injured arm in the water because my feet are numb. Behind a large green urn meant for an over-sized, summer arrangement of potted plants, I hold the canoe steady and Hugo lifts Peter-Andrew inside onto the backseat, our coxswain.

To row, I have to hang over the side with the lip of the boat cutting me in half. At first, we are paddling in circles.

"Stop, stop, stop, stop, stop." The boat gracefully slows

its pirouette. Peter-Andrew is laughing so hard that I begin to get why the Peter part of him is still with us.

Hugo shifts and the canoe rocks like a baby's cradle. "Nobody move," I say. "I don't want to get wet again." Peter-Andrew begins counting a rhythm. "One...two...three," but we are still going in circles.

"Elmur, you have to paddle as hard as Hugo is. It has to be equal."

"Then Hugo has to lighten up his stroke," I rough-whisper back. "My arms aren't as long as his."

"Ok...una tiempo mas, Uno, dos, tres—"

We are going forward. We...are...going...forward, at least until I miss all but the surface of the water and spray Hugo behind me. Oh, the Spanglish obscenities.

"Shhhh," Peter-Andrew and I both say.

"It's cold."

"Tell me about it."

"Will you babies row before you tip us all in and I drown?"

"His mouth works fine," I mutter, and I know that it's both the Andrew and the Peter in Peter-Andrew who are complaining.

I like the lake in the daytime. Without the sun shining through the water, it turns impenetrable, like dark tinted glass. I hear the clang and bangs of life from the few inhabited houses carried over the smooth surface of water that is hemmed in by mountains. The dipping of the kickboards in and out of the water has become rhythmic. I can see right down to the cement-filled tires that hold the docks in place. The water is transparent with the sun. At night, the lake holds all its secrets.

We beach the boat at a dirt path that winds from the lake to the main road. Stella's house is third tier from the lake.

"Do you think her parents are back from the high school? How do we get the people out of the house if they are?" I ask.

Peter-Andrew dials. Of course Peter knows her number.

After just one ring tone, the phone is answered. The voice is anxious and barks hello with anticipation. "Stella?"

They're back, he mouths.

"This is a friend of Stella's. I know that you are looking for her. I think I just saw her at the Eureka Motel. You know the one in…um…Eureka, with her boyfriend. They were getting out of a car. I wouldn't say anything, normally, but you know special circumstances, and she is being so weird."

"Who is this," a deep male voice, this time.

"David Poole. I know her from soccer camp. I help out there sometimes."

"She's being so weird." I whisper and laugh.

Peter waves me off. You know, the "be quiet" wave.

"Yes, that's right. I don't know. I don't know. No, I'm not there now. Yeah, yeah...sure. Goodbye."

"Brilliant. Let's get up to the house and see what happens," says Hugo.

I stare through the lighted windows at the house. It's so bright inside. Everyone is running around. It's like the house is on fire. Motors start. A cop's siren blares and echoes. Lights revolve.

"Sweet," I say. "Good one on you, Peter."

Hugo, me, and Peter-Andrew in Hugo's arms (no guilt from Peter-Andrew being carried about) approach the house with a stealth known only to Native Americans. I touch the back doorknob, jiggle it a bit and then turn it with a trepidation that makes me feel like a hairball is in my stomach. It turns, I push the door inward. The three of us are at the threshold gawking, afraid to step inside.

"No alarm."

"Even if they have one, they wouldn't stop to set it."

"I shouldn't think they need one," I say as I glance in. The kitchen has a dated and "used" look to it, like my gran's cheap oak cabinets, and stained Formica counters. The kitchen table is in a corner nook with china-blue and white ruffle cushions. I smell a pot roast cooking. I wonder whether they are now saying to themselves, did you turn off the stove? What a day for them. They probably forgot they put it in. It's slow cooking.

Even with the room being ordinary, and the door open, we don't move. It's like some sort of time-travel portal. The opening feels like a door with a kitchen around it, like a set for a TV series, and if any of us step through it, a trap is triggered, and we have to fight our way out with weapons we don't possess, and carrying Peter-Andrew on our backs. Who knows what lies behind the ordinariness that's there to suck you in? Well, at least that is me. Hugo has no subconscious battles here. He walks straight in.

I take one step under the lintel and nothing bites my shoe. I take another. I am breathing Stella-rarified air. Who knew her house is no better than mine? I walk to the oven and turn it off. They won't remember. I'm afraid to lose Hugo, so I hurry to catch up.

The bedrooms are upstairs. hers is the first one we try. It's obvious because of all the digital shots of herself and her friends thumbtacked to her wall. Hugo dumps Peter-Andrew on a chair at the desk. "How long to and back do you think?"

"Forty minutes generally, but they have police cars."

"Half hour at most then."

Well here I am. People's lives are made or broken in this room. Thumbs up, thumbs down. I have been talked about here. While she sat on that very bed, she pronounced me lame. Even so, if she invited me into this inner chamber, I still would have come.

The space is conventional...bed...dresser...desk...closet. Her clothes are on the floor. The bed is unmade. There's no beauty here. The bedspread is past its sell-by date. The furniture doesn't match, and it's scratched.

The room is ordinary enough though, nothing you'd look twice at, but power abides here. It's in the details of what is not in this space. She has no make-up mirror that magnifies facial flaws in order to paint them away. She doesn't wear make-up. She likes the way she looks even if she isn't beautiful. She might call herself interesting.

There are no posters of sun signs, Capricorn, Libra, Cancer...Sagittarius. Nothing telling her she is positive, full of energy and adventurous, honorable, honest, trustworthy, truthful, generous, and sincere. That's what my astrological poster in my room says. It also says that we December babies root for underdogs. That's because we *are* the underdogs.

There are no pictures that say "persevere" or "let the sunshine in." She doesn't need a daily pep talk from her walls. She doesn't have any video games. She doesn't live here, in here. She lives out there, and from that are all the pictures. Millions of photos of her and friends as a wall mosaic. Drawn to the life skills in them, I walk towards the photos. So many different people, and Stella is with them all, doing things, lots of things. I stare at her in each of the shots.

This is what I crave, her happy pictures.

"Why is she so horrible to me if she has all this?" I ask the air, or any gods who may be listening.

Hugo stands by me.

"She's in every picture. There are at least a hundred pictures. Narcissistic much," I mumble.

"What do you never ask a narcissist?" Peter-Andrew asks. "Would you like to get to know me? Get it? It's all about them."

"Yep, good one." I turn to scan the mess all over the room. "Anywhoo, how can we tell if she's been here?"

"Looks like she could have. She came for stuff and got out quick," says Hugo.

I turn back to the pictures. "We need to look for clues to her whereabouts." I study the picture of herself and her boyfriend. He's in his volunteer firefighter's outfit, and he's carrying her in his arms, and they are both laughing like they are the two happiest people in the world, and that's why I wanted to be Stella.

Hugo looks at what I'm looking at. "There's a whole lot of pictures with him."

"Brian Regan, with an "R."" He wasn't injected. Maybe Peter-Andrew is on base. Maybe she is with him at a hotel. "Where are they?" I am soaking in the details of each print of the hundred-picture wall.

"There's a lot of pictures of her and Brian in this place. Where is that?" I tug six pictures from the wall.

A very nearby German Shepard-type bark halts our conversation and helps us remember what room we are in.

"Do they have a dog?" I am now whispering to Hugo. "Would this be considered breaking and entering if we didn't break anything or, or take anything? God, maybe the police knew all along that the phone call was a fake. They all have been waiting around a corner, with a lookout saying, they've gone in, and now we are surrounded."

The dog barks again. The pot roast smells delicious. I wonder if they'll feed me in jail because the cinnamon tortillas are wearing off. Hugo shoves me into the closet. I apparently am the VIP. Nope, I'm the person that gets us in trouble.

"I'll tell them I stopped by to help," he says.

I'm in a closet, again, looking for anything that will help me battle my way out. Nothing but clothes and shoes. Dear God, this girl is boring. At least I'm not boring. I keep her entertained anyway.

I hear the bedroom door open. I squat with my butt against the back wall and with one hand down in front of me like I'm on the front line and am ready to burst from my slot. I am knee height and that's what I'll go for, their knees. I wait and watch the closet door for movement. I try to breathe lightly. The door does open, and I spring out like a confined twisted wire. I almost take Hugo down, almost. Well, I make him grunt anyway.

The big guy picks up my body with my legs still in motion.

"It's ok," he says as he puts me down.

"What gives?" I ask. I look towards the door that I knew had opened. The brace girl, looking all bumpy in weird places, is watching me.

Chapter Fifteen

Alice Norton is one of those "not-quite" people. Not quite pretty, not quite blonde, not quite tall, and not quite skinny. She is also not quite a ghost, but almost. I've never seen her full of emotion. Her brown eyes always look like she's in pain.

I jump at her sudden manifestation. "Geez, what are you doing here? How did you get in? Oh."

Duh.

We stare at each other, a strange grouping in the middle of Stella's house, in the heart of Stella's bedroom. The world has gone very weird.

"You know where she is don't you, Alice? You're leveraging up. You're spying on us."

Into the uncomfortable scene, Hugo says, "If she is a spy? Why isn't she spying instead of standing in front of us?"

"Whatever." I say that when I'm upset with myself, and the only way to cover-up is schnauzer-like. Growl or nip, I gotta save face. Anyway, I still couldn't figure her out. Why IS she here?

She glances around the room, and at the picture wall. She's never been here either. Of course she hasn't. This is a place that only a few of the chosen have been invited. That isn't Alice.

"What are you guys doing?" Besides leaving fingerprints?" She asks.

"Could ask you the same."

She doesn't answer. I want to point out that we don't have all the time in the world to gab or gawk in the middle of Stella's room, in the center of Stella's house, but I've already been snarky.

"I saw you get into the canoe. I live one house down from the hotel."

"They are going to be back soon, from a wild-goose-chase," I say.

"Then, maybe we all should take a souvenir and get out."

I like Alice a whole lot more as she walks over the closet, scrapes some hangers along a wooden dowel, and says, "I think I will have this."

She pulls out a royal blue t-shirt. She holds it up to herself. I read "King Me." There are checkers pieces screened onto the front of the shirt. It's so perfect as a "borrow."

"What about you?" she asked me.

I walk to her desk. I open a drawer with so much force that all the contents hit the front of it and then roll back like a wave. I shuffle through the pens and index cards and old IPods until I find a permanent marker. Black. Back at the pictures, I pick one and draw a low wall on the bottom half of the photo. On top of the wall, I sketch staring eyes, and then a nose hanging over the wall. Four fingers cling to the top of the wall on each side of the head. I over the top, I write, 'Kilroy was here,' and then Hugo takes the pen from me.

"Should we see if Stella's diary is here?"

Everyone laughs. If she had one, it was probably locked in a safe. I wish mine was. I stuff the pen in my pocket, and then I take a petite, gold-colored trophy, with a soccer ball glued on top that has "participant" written on it. I want to remember the time in which Stella was less than average.

"Vamanos," says Hugo.

Outside Alice and I walk the beach to her house. Hugo brings Peter-Andrew in the boat. "I smell smoke. She hasn't burned anything else down in my name, has she?" I hear another cop siren. It's hard not to look for cover.

When Hugo arrives at Alice's front door, carrying Peter-Andrew, Alice just walks across a mat and the door lock clicks. As she gets closer to the door, it opens. Ghost Alice has ghost friends. I glance at Peter-Andrew. This is his sort of thing. Whatever, this is anybody's sort of thing. Hugo, Peter-Andrew and I are awed-silent. The door is enough, but inside the place looks like a casino-owning Nez Perce might live there. It's a millionaire, custom-made, rustic lodge. They must have chopped through a forest for enough logs. I stare a moose head right in the eye as I pass underneath him. My bad self.

"Eloise?" Alice calls.

Kaiser had to sell our souls for the technology that enabled him to do that.

Alice darts a glance at me and Hugo. She's so uneasy looking that I think we are in the wrong house or something.

"Eloise," she calls out louder. "My voice isn't always out there enough," she explains.

"That's not a problem Elmur has," pipes up Peter-Andrew. I think again, *who is that coming from?*

"What can I do for you?" The body-less words in a home make me jump, *creepy.*

"What can we have to eat?"

"Scanning refrigerator. Looks like turkey sandwiches."

"Ok?" Alice asks us.

We nod in unison. Vague nods. We'd agree to anything.

"Thanks Eloise, in my bedroom please."

I widen my eyes at Hugo as I pass him to follow Alice.

We walk single file up the smooth, half-a-log pine stairs.

My hand slides over the glossy handrail as I ascend. In Alice's bedroom my foot SINKS INTO a soft taupe carpet. Alice's room is the best hideout an outlaw could hope for. I could live here forever. It has a gaming corner with a special wood floor for virtual play. The bed is fluffier than angel food cake. Seriously, she must never sleep in that perfect, lacy bed. It's a kipped-out room with everything anyone would want to watch or play with. It's the booty of supreme bribes...or...or...it's the promise of a mother's loving set-up for excellent friend-bait. Either way, sign me up. Peter-Andrew is put in a chair and plays with remotes. A ceiling to floor screen turns on.

"The vandalism will cost the city thousands of dollars. The police are not sure if this is tied to the other events around the town. They are proceeding with the assumption that it is."

I do what I do when there is nothing I can do. I step into the virtual circle, put on the goggles, and turn them on. Only to have Hugo rip them off my head.

"Hey."

"Time to be in real-time."

"Real-time has a lot to be desired right now."

A knock at the door. It opens. "Darling, Ellen said you were here and with friends." Alice's mom has a beautiful face, one that looks only sort of like Alice. I can see that Alice grabbed all the wrong genes.

Alice's mom has a wall-to-wall, gracious smile that she is beaming on us; so I'm thinking the stuff in the room is mostly friend-bait. I glance at Alice in her brace and figure that bribery is also at play in this room. Both Peter-Andrew and Hugo snap to attention.

"I'll go and bring up the sandwiches," the mother continues to gush. Right now, this woman would give us, as Alice's guests, her life and her heart. "It's so cold out. Why don't I bring up some hot chocolate? With peanut butter cookies." Her light and shiny hair, and her scent, roses, leave the room. We stare after her as if an angel has glimmered and disappeared.

Alice is…well, used to it all.

I rarely feel sorrier for someone else than myself, but this is pretty close. Imagine just missing all that perfection.

"I'm going to take back the canoe and get the wheelchair," says Hugo.

"Wait until we eat," says Alice, and I can hear the pure harmony that is in her mom's voice. I'd never really noticed how Alice sounds, mostly because she doesn't speak much. With a voice like that, Alice should talk more often.

"This is the best room I've ever seen. Your mom is all the good moms poured into one," I gush.

"Mi casa, su casa," she says and blushes as she glances at Hugo.

As I wander, picking up stuffed animals, and staring up at a six-foot giraffe, I ask, "Why did you follow us? I mean I'm glad and all…"

"Looking for opportunity."

I have to think about that. I always thought that Alice didn't feel. She is too colorless to have very deep emotions. Now that I see that she has everything, and if everything isn't enough, she can get more, I really see that she is all alone, two headsets, one Alice.

"I saw Stella run," she is telling me. "I heard your name over the loudspeaker. Two and two make four."

There I had been all my life thinking that it was me and Andrew, that nobody saw me, or if they did, judged me badly, but now I have two people stepping up to help. I mean they just appeared. Of course, I have to ask her why.

"Remember in seventh grade when the teacher was going to let out a few people to wash down the side of the gym and I was in my brace, and in the end the last slot was between Stella and I, and she said that I couldn't do it because I'd rust and then everyone would call me rusty corsets. Then when I tried out for cheerleader in eighth grade, Amanda said that if I won, she could grab the bars of my brace and shake me like a pom-pom."

I can see now why the brace had made Alice quiet. It's amazing, the magic of Stella's world and of the worlds of the people like her.

"Why help Elmur though? She said that you need more pizzazz to be a good brace girl," says Peter-Andrew.

"Whaat! I…I…" I trip over my tongue like I have clown shoes tied onto it. I glare at Peter-Andrew. He is injected, but he could have tried harder to keep quiet. I wait for the fallout. There is always fallout, and I'm down for two.

"She's right," Alice says and smiles at me. "I always thought you were pretty smart. You probably don't remember that you walked up to Amanda and punched her in the stomach" She touches my shoulder, a light touch, but I can feel it.

Her mom arrives with food, and I smell chocolate. These people are awesome. Her mom must be used to awkwardness in Alice's acquaintances because she just keeps walking and talking.

"Alice, bring that table over here. It is so nice to have you all here. Isn't it, Alice? We have a pool table in the basement, if you like pool. Alice is a great player. Do you all like to cross country ski? She does that. It's really too bad it's still cold out. Alice has been driving the boat since last summer. We could all use less snow and more warmth, couldn't we? We do have enough hot chocolate. That makes the cold easier."

She's like a rich Andrew's mom. Alice's mom is trying hard to make Alice new friends. When she 'leaves us to it,' and we start eating, Alice actually says, "I'm sorry. It's just that she wants you to like me."

"I believe that I like you even without the chocolate, and the stuff."

Alice smiles at me. The one thing about people who tell the truth, you can always believe them.

Peter-Andrew and Hugo glance at each other.

Hey! I can be a not-terrier in an "Elmur" sort of way.

And then Alice laughs. No one has ever heard her laugh. It is a beautiful laugh. It makes her brace disappear. I tell her that.

"You like my room," she says.

"Who wouldn't? Friend-bait?"

Alice laughs again. "God. That is exactly what it is. Score." We fist pump.

"What about that painting? Who did that?"

"My older sister. She is very gifted. If you all notice, the face of the dog is perfect. The artist loves dogs. My face looks like I just farted or something. I keep it because that was my dog when I was little."

"Pre-brace?" *Dear God, did I just say that?* The brace does suck. It's almost a full metal jacket, clear up to her ears. Her short hair is rubbed uneven in the back by the hard plastic headrests attached to the metal ring around her neck. There's a plastic chin rest too. One flat pole in front disappears into the neck of her shirt, two flat poles arch under her shirt and over her shoulder blades in the back. It looks heavy.

"My little sister is the star pitcher on the softball team. I was supposed to be the boy. I heard my mom say that."

"And middle child."

"Actually, my name isn't Alice. I like to use different names. Mom never knows what name to call me. She does try to keep up. My Dad tells her to call me by my real name. She tells him they must be patient. My Dad's motto is if you're in the audience, you're clapping for someone else." She laughs again. "I used to want to be extraordinary, for attention, like my sisters, for my Dad. Now, I am extraordinary. I have people staring at me all the time. I have people telling me I'm so brave, or gutsy, or amazing, but all I know is how I look to people. The brace girl. Everywhere I go, everything I do, I have to prepare mentally for the pity in their eyes or the what-happened-to-her gawking. None of us are comfortable. I am brave and gutsy, but only enough to walk into a room." Alice takes in our startled faces and then starts apologizing. She and I both know that one utterance over the socially acceptable line, and we are declared incontinent.

"How are you "Alice" in school?" asks a fascinated Hugo.

"The power of being so special."

"Why Alice?" he continues.

"Alice, as in Lewis Carroll. My favorite books. I want adventure. Who cares about standing out in a crowd? Pfffttt." She snaps her fingers. "Just being ordinary again would be fine with me. I can clap happily and long and live under the wire." Ghostly Alice is becoming more substantial with every word.

"So, when do you get that heavy thing off and become a real girl?" I ask.

"Oh man, after three years, with only one hour a day out of it… soon; this summer, I think."

"Getting out from behind bars." I say.

She laughs again. I love that laugh. It is invigorating. It kind of bubbles and rises. It is light without darkness. Alice is so not who I thought she was.

"This room needs some wear," I say standing. Hugo grabs my arm to sit me back down.

"When I saw you in the canoe, I knew where you were going." Alice stood and walked to a closet. "Anyway, I think I can help." With a flourish she pulls open two white doors. Inside were weapons, of all destruction.

Man, I was SO wrong about the curious Alice in Wonderland. She is a player. Looks like we are about to play for real, but with fake weapons.

Chapter Sixteen

Alice, standing in front of the closet of my dreams, is here to help, to share, for no reason except that she is nice, and she is adventure depleted. Her face is open, and she is happy to please as I approach her closet, my Mecca. My hand shakes as I reach for a saber. I underestimated Alice big time. She probably asked for a saber and got the whole set. Lucky stiff. I mean, I didn't mean stiff, as in can't bend or anything like that.

Within my fingertips are a Scottish claymore, a rapier, a battle axe, an elven sword, and throwing stars. I wrap my fingers around the hilt of a saber. It is beautiful with its Celtic designs along the shaft. I lift it from its cradle and hold it before my eyes. My touch registers to my brain that the weapon is too light. I pick up a throwing star. The weight is wrong. *What?*

"They wouldn't let me have the real thing. Sorry. They have carbon fiber cores which is swathed in foam and coated with latex."

I shrug my shoulders. I smile my best smile because the saber's a pleasure to hold even if it is fake. I swing it. It's exceptionally light, easy to handle. I turn and assault the closet door. I pretend to counter-parry, riposte. I circle the weapon to disengage. The weapon is perfect in my hand, so free of weight. I feel real with it.

"It sure looks real." I turn it over and inspect the Celtic, swirled engraving along the hilt. The sword is becoming a natural extension of my arm. "We'll look armed to the teeth," I say.

Peter-Andrew has rolled over to the closet at hyper speed. Alice hands him the battle axe.

"Let's go find her," he says while also figuring balance.

I pull the pictures I took from Stella's wall from my pocket and spread them on a table. I point at each of them with the saber, because I can. "There were a bunch of pictures of this place and of them together. Where is this? Anybody know?"

Alice opens a drawer to a study desk and comes back with a magnifying glass. Is there anything this girl doesn't have?

"Thought I recognized it. See this sign?"

We all lean in.

"Whittling," Hugo says.

"It's so tiny. How did you see it?" I wanted to finish with "bionic eyes," but for once I bit my tongue. Funny how like and respect make that easier.

"I've seen it a million times. My dad is the camp leader. With all girls in my family, it's his boy fix. Know what else? James Peterman, the custodian, is out of town."

"Related to Michael Peterman Stella's devotee? Probably gets free back rubs."

"Yes."

"Also not injected," I inject.

"Why so many pictures there do you suppose?" Asks Hugo

"She is a member of the Female Friends to the Boy Scouts."

"Of course she is."

"You a boy scout Hugo?" I ask. "Andrew went to camp once."

"I was," said Peter-Andrew. "The camp is a couple of acres of trees and brush and plants, a few cabins, and itty-bitty latrines. Best thing though is there are Hawkin Thompson .50 cal black powder rifles, Anschutz M64MPR22 target rifles, scopes and some Savagemark Shotguns, and archery equipment."

"All the girl scouts have are glue guns."

We are all quiet. We are always playing defense.

"Got anything else in this room?" I ask Alice. "The cops have Andrew's laser scope pellet gun." My hand practically slaps me as I cover my mouth. I'm not going to look, but I hear the Andrew in Peter-Andrew squeak. He is so going to kill me when this is all over, if I'm not already dead or in jail.

I remember the saber in my hand. I point it at Hugo's throat. "This will work. I mean, it's not like we can really stab them anyway. We can poke and smack.

"While they shoot us," says Peter-Andrew.

"Guys, I don't want to get you in any more trouble or shot—"

"Can it, Elmur," they say in unison.

"We have to get in and get out. We have to create holes for ourselves," says Hugo.

"Misdirection," Peter-Andrew and I say at the same time.

"We want the ball back, what do we need?"

"A loose ball," says Alice.

Hugo smiles. We are all his little grasshoppers.

"We can enhance and add," Peter-Andrew says slowly like an idea, any idea is foreign to him. "Pepper bombs, flash powder, potato cannons with silencers, and some modified water guns. The water is cold. The air is cold." Peter-Andrew is looking real earnest as he warms to his ideas.

"How about a bag of snakes." I glance to Hugo.

"Yes, create, divide and conquer," says Alice. "And then, man on man, the swords look real. You said it yourself, Laura," says Alice.

"Again, unless once they see us, and they shoot us with a couple of Hawkin Thompson .50 cal black powder rifles," I add.

"Would they really shoot us do you think? Isn't it hard to actually shoot someone?"

"People do though don't they, in schools. Bet you wrote in that book that you'd like to shoot someone," Peter-Andrew says.

"Yeah, you. I did not write anything like that. I don't know, Alice. It's crazy out there. They are crazy."

"The strategy in uneven skirmishes is to wear the opponent down." says Hugo. "The play field is large, lots of running. Space and movement and motivation and planning, that's what we have, and surprise. It's hard to get a person if they have space to get around you. Even with guns. How many can aim? There are trees."

"We are not soup-can targets. We are big, easier to hit. You know, lots of them have been hunting from the age of ten. Gran would say it's an accident waiting to happen."

"Ok, there's risk. We minimize that. What exactly is our objective?" asks Alice.

"Get the tell-all diary," says Peter-Andrew.

"How do we find it?"

"Infiltration and surprise," says Hugo.

"We need helmet lights or night goggles," I say.

"Night goggles, the lights will make us targets," says Peter-Andrew.

"Who has night goggle connections?" I ask.

"Easy," says Peter-Andrew. "All you need are 9V batteries, an infrared LED from old TV remote controls, some wire with a battery clip and gel."

Peter can't keep the Dr. Frankenstein in Andrew down. He modifies everything that comes close to him.

So it begins with a check-in call to Gran. That takes a while. I assure her that I am fine and have a job given to me by Principal Kaiser to help find myself; and that I have help and am staying the night at Alice's. Gran trusts me. I've never given her a reason not to. A few other calls, and then next is a visit to Walmart in Alice's self-driving car which is so cool that Peter-Andrew won't get out of it. We are going down in style.

"You don't happen to have a 3D printer lying around?" Asks our injected one.

We buy flour and salt. Plastic wrap and rubber bands. Three water guns and bike tubes. Stuff to make backpack modifications for water. We get a bunch of TV remotes.

Alice's mom lets us know that they are all leaving for a fundraiser they are hosting. Alice is exempted because she has guests. I am Andrew's surgical nurse as he gets into the pressure chamber of a water gun. I hand him the hacksaw from Alice's garage. "Be careful not to damage the rubber inside," he says to me. He teaches this stuff. I give him the Philips screwdriver, to remove the end clamp. He layers donut-shaped bike tubes onto the chamber and then puts the clamps back on. The increased thickness of the chamber increases pressure. This gun has a nozzle selector. We just have to remove it to get a shotgun blast.

When we finish three guns, we start one of the water-gun backpacks. We use five-gallon, solar-powered, camp showers, some tubing, tubing barbs, couplers, and tubing clamps. The water backpacks are filled with iced down water that has been mixed with pepper. That spice is cheap. I sew carrier bags for the potatoes to use with the potato gun.

We clean off the table to start the smoke-pepper bombs. They will help in case of flashlights, and phones with flashlights

To make a smoke bomb, you use flour and salt and baking powder, water, and pepper. We are all doing this in a kind of assembly line. Alice mixes the stuff in a bowl. I'm in charge of making a wet spot in the middle of a paper towel where I put the stuff from the bowl. Andrew ties the ends of the paper towels with rubber bands. We are the A-Team. Cue the music.

I'm the most interested in the night goggles. He was going to go for welders' glasses, with blue and red theatrical gels glued onto the lenses and some LED lights connected to a battery taped to the frame. With Alice's encouragement, Andrew decided to get a little fancier with a headset and dash camera put together connected to a phone charger. Also, we didn't know how to get theatrical gels.

Alice has Internet-Eloise retrieve and print a copy of the campground map. It is rudimentary so Alice and Peter try to remember more details. By midnight we have a map, potato cannons, homemade bombs, modified water guns, and carbon swords. We have four people, they have…don't know. Also, I don't know if crazy is good for our side or theirs.

Alice's room looks like a munitions factory and smells like rotten eggs. We open the bedroom windows and start cleaning up.

"It won't happen just like the play," Hugo says as he coaches us. "You have to keep thinking. We all have to interact to control the variables, to control the outcome. "It's going to be about what you have to do, not about what you can do."

I smile winsomely. "And we keep playing until the last play just before the last buzzer."

He doesn't take the bait, but keeps on going, "You have to be able to block out bad thoughts. You, especialmente you."

"Mwah?" I give him a sour face.

"What about your video games. How do you stay focused?"

"She doesn't," pipes in Peter-Andrew.

I stick out my tongue. "First of all, in video games, DYING is temporary. There are as many chances as you need. There is no pressure. My real body is not a part of play."

"Still, do you figure your virtual self will win?"

"Of course."

"Because?"

"Because I can make mistakes and come back, and learn, and do it better the next time." I almost swallow the last word. "Whatever," I say. "Go away."

We pack our weapons.

When I was in kindergarten, when I still thought myself fine, I liked the people I met for too long and too well. I didn't see until too late that just because you like someone doesn't mean they will like you back or ask you over. That's not how it goes. I didn't get it. I thought, I like you. I'm being nice to you. What's the matter? Reality of life made me sad and then mad. Packing weapons now, I am mad and sad. Reality sucks. Socialization sucks, except sometimes I get to use smoke bombs and fireworks and paint guns. *Stunning Stella here we come.*

Chapter Seventeen

Alice goes to the bathroom to disrobe out of her brace. "This will be more than an hour, but—"

"Pfffttt, with it," I finish. I note the brace lying there like an insect exoskeleton leaning in the corner. It has a curve-lipped, leather pelvic girdle that would look really cool over a body stocking, but without the steel poles. Actually, it looks frightening in a steampunk sort of way. I tell her so, because that's what I do, and I'm glad when she giggles again even if it's a cringing sort of sound. She is really not used to laughing at it.

She puts on the mail shirt she has. She is used to carrying steel weight on her body. It's like metal silk, and I want one and regret that there are not two. I'm fairly sure that I will need more protection than that anyway. Superpowers are needed to defeat Stella Miller. It's short of a miracle that we found her at all…Kaiser.

Behind me there's a battle between Peter and Andrew over costuming. Andrew wants to wear the helmet from a set of armor. Peter won't let him put it on his head. It is funny. His arms are like frozen. Andrew is an athletic slacker, and so is Peter. Even match. How they end up with the hat even

129

half on, I'll never know. It is all in their head, and their minds are merging ever closer. I wonder if they'll be clear-headed enough to do their job, say if one of Peter's friends come barreling at us.

My bangs press down into my eyes from the bike helmet I wear. Alice also has a bike helmet. Bike helmets protect your head if the road rises up to meet it, but what about bullets?

Dressed, we make our way to the water. The Lake is super quiet in May anyway and at midnight empty. Most of the houses are seasonal, so no one is at home. We thought about taking the car, but we'd have to call her parents and come up with a story to get it, and we figured that the cops would have cars, and that they will be watching the road. The camp entrance is literally on the road that circles the lake.

Also, no one has boats. Anything that floats is still in storage. One thing we finally have in our favor is that Alice has a boat house on the lake with all kinds of floating things in it. Alice's mother called several times through the night to check and see if we are alright. They went to a Cinco de Mayo fundraiser that they are hosting. Which is mostly bust as people are either talking about the injections or home with their kids that were injected. Her mom said they'd all be home soon after clean up; and did Alice need her sisters to come home earlier as it is getting late? Um, no.

We hope that by the time we row to Camp Harrison, Team Stella will all be asleep, and if they wake, they will be groggy. We have to be quiet, so we will take the fishing boat with the motor as far as Huckleberry Island. From there, we have peeking distance to Camp Harrison beach. We will assault the beach from two kayaks and a canoe, and we hope to find it unoccupied. We tie the canoe with a kayak in it to the back of the fishing boat. Another kayak joins us in the main vessel. I will take the canoe with our "defensive team" in it. That would be Peter-Andrew and all the stuff we have made. Alice and Hugo take a kayak each so we can scatter later if we need to, dividing up their defense.

There is no risk on the water, no other boats creating swells and traffic. The boat skims easily. I hear the bow cut the water. There is little moon light, God's fingernail Lots and lots of stars though, and the Milky Way, and The Big Dipper. We are wearing the night vision goggles. We have to get used to them and to looking through the camera.

We stop at the island and tie up to the dock of the only house there. Camp Harrison beach is about seven hundred feet away. At the center of the beach is a pole the shape of a cross, with flag wires that attach to the extended arms and to the base. It stands like the yardarm of a sail. Through our improvised goggles, it looks bleached white. Ghost trees begin about fifty yards up the sand. The area is still clear of Boy Scout stuff, changing tents, boats of any size. This is good. We discussed what to do if we found boats. Sink them? NO! Move them to use as protection? NO! "What about if they have no oars?" I asked. I felt smart.

We plan to tie the canoe with Peter-Andrew and the potato canons in it to the dock. He is our water defense when we return and are possibly being pursued. He will carve out time for us to get into the boats.

Hugo lifts Andrew into his final boat. I jump as one of the canons in the bottom of the canoe falls on its side. It's time like these that try a man's soul. Funny how words that you hear in English class have more power in real life situations.

A line in the sand. That moment when you have to play to win or die. I read a real-life story about a lady who had bumps all over her body, kind of like a pseudo-cancer and even before that her mom used to tell her she was ugly, and when the bumps arrived, oh man. And so, she hid from people all her life, and hardly went anywhere. Then one day she is actually hit by a flipping car, icing on the cake. Lucky to still be alive, she decides that, what the hell, she's going to go out and do things, see the world, jump into the pit, and ignore the flipping monsters that live there. Nothing left to lose. Play to be seen or die, that's what the Aztecs say.

We are getting closer to the beach. I hear a Hugo's boat touch sand, and then Alice's. Peter-Andrew and I pull up to the dock, and our bow knocks hollowly against the wood. Our landing party sounds without depth.

I inhale and blow out through my mouth. Could be an army in the trees, waiting. I mean Andrew is controlled by Peter, and Peter is an insider. If we are the offense going in, Hugo says put space between the three of us to make us seem bigger. Use the whole field so they have to find us, come to us. For sure though, they are going to be one aggressive defense.

We don't talk right away but listen for the voices of others. All we hear is disturbed water sucking at our hulls. Through the camera, the pine trees and the bushes look like we are in an apocalypse. Good. I'm used to working in foreign territory with goggles on. Hugo is out of his boat and coming over, Alice too. Peter-Andrew scans the pines as we unload. We hide two kayaks and tie the canoe. We tie it loosely.

The sand is hard. There are pockets of white that is snow. Weathered wooden benches form a square in front of the flagpole. Inside the square is a stone fire ring. A three feet in diameter log stretches a good ten feet across the upper left part of the beach. Smaller logs and spaced vertical posts, which probably hold up a canvas ceiling during the summer, define the perimeter of the upper area. There is also a carved wooden entrance arch that says, "Waterfront." Leave it to authority to state the obvious. Behind that the woods begin. There is a shed by the lake on the right and a porta potty. We are lucky. There is a safety flood light over the beach area and there is a well-made storage hut with exterior electrical outlets. Bring the tennis ball launcher, a last minute add-on. Excellent start meaning ends-in-failure.

We run cable from Peter-Andrew's canoe up the beach. We decided on three lines of defense. Because of the gully that runs astride the dirt road from the beach up to the main road, our pursuers will have to come after us on the dirt road. The gully is part of team Elmur. Our man-on-man defense, the dirt bombs, will guard the road. Our offensive linemen, a curtain of fireworks will light up the waterfront sign. Our left tackle is the auto, tennis ball launcher from Alice's tennis court.

I am in the dirt arranging bombs. I am close to the main road. It is dark here, very dark, and creepy. I think of kids with guns, but I also think of bears. I want to work faster, but Hugo told us a thousand times to keep our minds in the game and on what we are doing. He said it to me a thousand times more after I told him that my mind is creative and wanders. He said it to me again before he and Alice left to get the tennis ball machine. He would have left Alice to help set up the explosives, but after spending so much time with Andrew, I am better at wiring things.

As I'm working with the various bombs, my entire body is relieved when I hear the creak of the wheels of the tennis ball machine. Hugo and Alice aim it at the road while I run more wire from them to the two car batteries in the canoe.

I put smoke and stink bombs into the lower pockets of my cargo pants and then paint gun bullets into every other possible place. Alice is carrying a backpack full of water and a high-pressure water gun. She took that instead of a paint gun because she said that she didn't know how to aim. I sling one over her head anyway and stuff her pockets. Hugo has the same.

Peter-Andrew has the explosives plunger, and a water gun backpack and a paint gun. "I'm a sitting duck bobbing on the water." he said to me when we were allocating ammo.

"You know most of them," I said back. And he didn't say, not in this body, which I say is telling. Anyway, I know they both wouldn't miss being in the center of an apocalypse.

"If anything happens, you set off the explosives early and then you've got to paddle out of here," I say to him. "Remember, you can walk. You can walk and run. God. This is…without equal."

I turned to face my own fears and Stella.

At the beginning of the trees, Hugo descends the short hill to the creek at the bottom. Alice keeps to the road, and I am in between them at the lip of the road. We have walkie-talkies.

"Ready?" That was Hugo. "Remember that they can't see you. Best thing is to slip through them without sound. Use rocks as an extra player. Throw it way to the side. If they are going to shoot, have them shoot at nothing."

We get to the main lake road. Another carved wooden sign says, "BEWARE road crossing." Alice and I grimace at each other. "It was for a carving badge," I whisper. At the crossroads there is also an old rowboat propped on its side and painted with the Boy Scout crest and the words, "Be prepared."

"The boy scouts should have done the injections." Alice says.

The larger, open road is no man's land, unprotected, nothing to hide behind. The plan is for Hugo to go first while I have his back, then me, then Alice. So far, we have had it easy, saving the worst. Hopefully we have the advantage of surprise, because they have all the rest.

"Going," my walkie-talkie chirps. I have my paintball gun at my shoulder to back him up. I see the ghost of his body. I wait. My turn. I run across and then Alice.

As we steadily move forward, I'm on the path and Alice and Hugo are in the woods. They are making so much noise, I suggest that we walk on the path together and spread back out when necessary. We've seen nobody. We are west of the mess hall that is located at the front of the camp by the entrance. I'm glad we are together. Even together, my hands are so tight on the paintball gun, that I am getting cramps. I feel the sword against my leg. We search the darkness for popup people, white shirts, or even for a faint glint of a gun barrel pointed at us from the brush.

A real game is terrifying. The breeze lifts the hairs on my skin. The smells remind me that I'm not home on my couch with the action safely on my screen. My nostrils fill with the magnified scent of dirt and pine. Each step is begrudged. My mind wants to react to the fear it is feeding itself. The desire to turn around is overwhelming. My hands sweat and my pits. I feel warm and cold. My tense body waits for pain and flinches at any touch by a branch. I wonder how Alice is doing. She is at the tail of our group. Maybe she is becoming a ghost of herself again. I don't know if she will be dependable when the time comes and that makes me feel sick for both of us.

She told us about how her mom tried to make her feel normal by taking her out of school one day to try skiing with the brace on. The lift guy slowed the chair down to barely moving so she could sit down. The brace tilted back against the seat, metal to metal, like a plank. The halo around her neck was shoved up against her jaws. How is that normal? The thing about people is that they have good intentions, but no common sense. Like the time her mom took her to ride a horse. Alice fell off in the first minute. She and her brace crashed to the ground. I shouldn't worry about Alice so much. Look what ridiculousness she has been through. God, she got back on that horse. She is one of the bravest people I know.

The trail according to the map comes into the camp north of the populated area and skirts the rifle and archery range. We know that there are twenty-seven latrines with no doors on them. We know that within a few yards of each other are the dining hall and the leather, basket, and wood carving area, which is full of cutting and scraping and burning tools. Also, give yourself a three-minute walk from the Dining Hall, there is the shop area with every tool in it known to man. The boy scouts could hold their own, should aliens invade.

As we walk on, I notice to the left, a platform.

"Archery," Alice whispers.

I almost hear the 'fffttt' sound of disturbed air as I imagine an arrow is being launched. My body tenses even more. I will need a chiropractor. There is no sound here. Next door is the rifle and muzzle loader range.

"Let's check it and see if the guns are there," says Hugo. The shooting area has a roof and platform. Along the edge of the platform are body shooting sleds. Just off the platform and in front of the carpets are rifle holders. I look out to the wooden cutouts of pigs, deer, and chickens.

"I want to be a boy scout."

"You can now," says Alice.

The gun lockers, three of them are against a single back wall. The locks are sprung, the doors hang open. The weapons are absent. I look at the indentations that should hold the rifles and muzzle loaders. They look like incredibly old coffins that's stuffing has molded around the bodies sleeping in them. I count them. Fifteen missing guns. Even the muzzle loaders, and who knows how to load those suckers...every Boy Scout here.

"Maybe we should go back," I say. "I mean, look at this. They are rabid-bat crazy."

"It's still four weeks to the first camp. Maybe the guns aren't here yet," says Alice.

"Then why are the doors open?"

"They came looking for them but didn't find them and left the doors open."

"Yeah, that has to be," I say glancing back over my shoulder as we walk away. I didn't believe myself, but added anyway, "Probably, the bows and arrows aren't out either."

Our feet meet with a camp road. Straight ahead is the marsh for nature badges. To the right down the road, the north showers, five outhouses—the blue spruce, pine, sequoia, aspen, and tamarack, so named I figure because all boys really want to do is hose down trees.

The dining hall is a hop skip and a jump to the right. It is the epicenter.

We still don't hear voices, maybe this will be a piece of cake. Sure, if the diary is kept outside the building, on the road.

"Should we stay together?" Alice asks.

I'm thinking that fear loves company and say, "Maybe they feel comfortable that no one is going to bother them."

The thought is not totally stupid, I think, until Alice says, "They have burned a sign and defaced the school."

Yup, totally stupid.

At the sound of a dry stick cracking, we flee like rabbits behind trees. My breathing is too heavy, and I try to slow it down. Another crack, I am searching the eerie woods. At first my head is darting here and there, but I tell myself again to slow down. My brain explodes when I hear the scramble of a body in the brush. I twist around and aim the paint gun. I'm about to shoot, but then see it's a deer. With a jump, it veers left. I let the gun drop, but I am shaken. So much for keeping my cool in the pressure of the game.

"You ok?" It's the walkie-talkie.

"Yeah, just a deer. Come out, come out, wherever you are."

We huddle on the dirt road. "A deer almost tackled me. He just missed me by a foot. I must have startled him. And him, me. My heart is still pounding. Should we have played that differently?"

"Good you didn't shoot."

"Yeah."

"Que Bueno, you are thinking all the time, putting your foot down inside the line, and we don't have the sound of the shot to deal with." Hugo patted me on the back. I take a deep breath.

Here we are chatting on the road. The nothing of the night has us beginning to relax. I think of Peter-Andrew. Is he bored? Is he talking to himself? Is he paying less attention now too? He has a walkie-talkie, but we haven't heard from him. Worst case scenario, if they've found him, Peter in the Peter-Andrew can switch sides. We'll just have to deal with that. Andrew wouldn't like it, but Andrew can't convince Peter that they can walk. The Peter-Andrew-model hasn't seen himself in a mirror, probably the Peter in Andrew doesn't know he's sharing. It might be like being schizophrenic, with one personality being dominant and all the personalities not knowing about each other.

"Still good there, Peter?" I have to check specifically.

"Quiet here," he replies. Ok, I feel better.

We stop when we see the first latrine that is on the road. "Anybody gotta go before we get into the car?" I quip. "Hey, you think they figured out how to turn on the water in the main building?"

As if to let me know, Stephanie Norton, trying to pull down her shirt and hold up a low watt flashlight, walks out of the semi-outdoor john, and here we are moseying down the road. Not sure if jumping into the trees and calling attention to ourselves, or freezing is our best option, we freeze out of pure indecision.

She is too busy talking to herself to see Hugo, or me, or Alice, or a log a foot in front of her. Down she goes, and then up she rises spitting muddy water, and still talking like she is two people. "You're an idiot. Can't you even walk? Me? You! You had to drink the whole glass before going to bed. What did you think your bladder was going to do, seal the opening until morning? I was thirsty! You deserve your face in the mud for dragging us out to, to a hole in the ground in the freezing cold. I had a headache. You can take a pill with three sips. You won't let me go home. You're a headache. You're an idiot." Perfect Steph is talking to herself like she has two heads; she sort of does, and maybe the second one is a hostile takeover. I fear she will sock herself.

A little tiny bit of me wants to see that, but that kind of thinking got the diary live.

"Whiner! Princess!" she says as she moves off to the dining hall.

I once watched a movie on Egyptian mummies. When a person dies a violent death, its spirit stays around. Nothing can make it go away. Evil magicians use incantations to control the dead body. They can make the desiccated spirit obey. An evil magician has been messing with Stephanie by the name of Stella.

"Did you see that? How many do you suppose are like that in there?" Alice whispers.

"And these people have guns?" I add.

"Why isn't Andrew like that?" whispers Hugo.

"He avoids conflict." It breaks my heart that Andrew has given over his body without a second word. Andrew is pragmatic. He knows that it will all be over. He's probably hidden deep in his hypothalamus, you know coordinating things like his nervous system, pituitary, body temp…all the homeostatic, technical stuff.

We hold back to let Steph gain yardage from us. As the sound of Stephanie fades, Alice says, "So the water is still turned off."

"Pero," says Hugo, "Probablemente hay people now awake que were asleep before she left."

"Who calls people "princesses" all the time? She's such a princess."

"Maddie Albright, black belt, all-school girl's wrestling champion," says Alice.

"OMG, that's right, and she calls Stephanie that because on the eighth-grade ski trip, Steph showed up in a matching ski outfit—pink spider jacket with pink boots and board and pants and hat and ribbons on her blonde braid."

"And a tiara glued on the front of her helmet."

"Maddie and Stella are very close," Hugo chimes in.

"Her henchman."

"Remember in fourth grade when she showed the class how to load a muzzle loader…powder, ball, ball starter, ramrod to seat it, percussion cap, nipple…she tossed that heavy gun around like a Civil War soldier."

"The girl has always had muscles."

"Now she is Stephanie."

"And she's beating up Steph on the inside."

"Steph likes herself. She'll get through it."

"I don't know. Perfect Steph has never taken hits like that." She's worse than Peter-Andrew. What we have to look forward to. Death, hellfire, and destruction.

Chapter Eighteen

We have made a tactical error.

As we arrive at the dining hall, we find that the Maddie-Stephanie was not as consumed with her inner demons as we thought. She must have the ears of an eagle scout, because she is waiting outside the door. Seeing us on the road confirms all her expectations. She goes all blitzkrieg. The multiple demons in her stream out. Like the Winter Wizard in the kid's Christmas cartoon, her eyes are spinning and in different directions. I hit the ground and am eating dirt and shaking like ice cream and milk in a blender. Hugo and Alice dive into nearby brush.

"While Alice and I decoy the revengeful herd of zombies about to come out the door into the trees—"

Yup that is what he said.

"Laura, you go in for the touchdown. Let them screen though you."

Not the screen play again!

I am afraid for many reasons, and not just because I watch movies on Egyptian mummies. Stephanie comes for us. No, seriously, she comes for us. She is possessed. I hear Hugo say the words, "Dios Mio," without the walkie-talkie.

Once Gran's friend's daughter came for a night. She had to be returned early. She thought Gran was poisoning her with the brown sugar Gran put on her oatmeal.

"Her brain just isn't right," Gran said. "Nothing to do with you or me. It's her neurotransmitters. They don't communicate."

There's only room for one voice in your head especially if THAT one is yapping at you all the time.

So we are waiting on the ground, Alice, Hugo and me, for Maddie-Stephanie and the bunch of freshmen the dining hall is regurgitating out its door. High school freshmen who, not long ago, and recent enough to spit and hit, were in middle school; who still just as soon spit on you as be nice; freshmen who are probably having uncommunicative neurotransmitters problems. We are here because of the national interest of peaceful co-habitation. Adults never get it right because the solutions are like pieces of broken glass, reflective of only one part of a whole.

And so it will be. Zombies verses humans. These are perfect zombies, who as humans, never did cool things like rescue blocks of ice from storm drains, or dig holes, just to dig. They were always on task and socially coherent, and they suck your blood. Being dead inside, the zombies always win.

As the screen door is shoved open by each person through it, it hits the wall behind, bam, bam, bam. My hand tightens on my paint gun. Maybe we should all, not just me, let them screen through. They can keep walking and looking in the dark forest, but what if they go to the beach and find Andrew.

Arrrrgggg.

We have night goggles, which are not useful in the auto-on perimeter lighting around the dining hall; the flood lights and then high-beam cell phone lights. Their pale faces are multiplying and spreading out. I taste salt from the sweat on my upper lip. I scrunch deep into the soil under me, while listening to the mumble of nearing voices and the shuffle of many feet on the dirt road.

I can't fire. That would give away my position. I'm not in a good place. Two are walking straight towards me. I mean, one, in about ten steps is going to use me as a carpet. Is this the part when I call the play blown, and I figure out what to do next?

They are coming, more slowly now though. They don't know what's out there. It could be cops, or their parents. In the light, I see that three, maybe four of them carry shotguns diagonally across their bodies.

Idiots, and you are going to shoot whom?

"Run diversion, Alice!" I hear in my earpiece. "Go in Elmur."

What, what?

Alice fires a round with her paint gun and then hot-foots it into the trees. Jason Anderson, frosh student rep. looking like death warmed over, Hattie Maitland, voted last year most likely to become a model, now looking like she stuck her finger into ten electrical sockets, and Joe Williams, quarterback potential and ladies' man who walks like the ape man cometh, follow her. Hugo, from down low, fires to guard her retreat. Jason spins like a Tasmanian devil. Hattie's no fool, she ducks. Joe takes her shot of purple paint in the face. Beautiful.

Now they are a bunch of really angry zombies, with their teeth gnashing. Hugo tosses out two stink bombs. The darlings explode at their zombie feet and send up a geyser of dirt, blinding the lot.

I'm watching all this with my mouth open. Hugo and Alice are bringing it. I forget I'm a player 'til my headgear squawks, "Rush the hole." I see Hugo disappear into the brush. The zombie hoard, smearing earth from their eyes, run after him. He is gone and then all the blood rushes from my brain.

"Rush the hole. Rush the hole," Hugo is screaming into the device in my ear.

With his voice still in my head, I scramble to my feet. I'm not coordinated yet, and I nearly trip over my fat feet. I haven't yet given my feet clear instructions. The door to the lodge is still open and my feet keep running to it. When I'm through it, I close and lock it. I'm leaning against it thinking; I'm here, and my worst nightmare smells like pepperoni pizza with a tinge of beer.

Crazy, drunk, hostile, fourteen-year-old zombies, what could be worse?

I'm glad they didn't turn on the lights as they left, that is until I take my first step away from the door and fall flat on my nose. My goggles fly off. I don't move. The only sound is my own heavy breathing. I smell the dust blow-back from the floor as I lie face down. Nothing stirs. There is no one about. I pat the floor around me, searching for the goggles, but they have flown the coup.

Turn on the lights. Where are the switches? By a door, idiot.

I crawl backwards in what I think is the way I came in until I hit a wall or something. Standing, and then feeling my way, I find a door. I hit the switch. I see a long room of brown planks and beams. On the center beam I read, "Trustworthy, Loyal, Helpful, Friendly, Courteous, Kind, Brave, Thrifty, Obedient, Cheerful, Clean, Reverent." At least the boy scouts are trying. "Clean," that's a good one. That's never in a Girl Scout manual. "Reverent." I mean, what does that mean exactly? The room is stuffy like a gym sock in the face, the smell of over-ripe fourteen-year-olds with fear-induced over-productive sweat glands. I know this because every year for the last two years the gym teacher gives a talk on deodorant use.

I count ten sleeping bags. Unless one or two are sleeping alfresco, ten untrustworthy, unloyal, unhelpful, unfriendly, uncourteous, unkind, and insane bodies are spending the night here. Five of them are after Hugo and Alice. Not sure about the other five.

God, where to begin looking in the mess of bottles and trash. I grab a bag and give it a shake down. I recite Hugo's football Bible to myself as I pick up the next bag.

"Defense and offense are taking the fight to the other team and not waiting. Surprise gives you the initiative. Surprised teams do stupid things."

I pick up the last bag and nothing falls out. So, zilch so far. No surprises.

"Ok, Ok, that's ok. Understand your assets." I spend a lot of video game-time looking for things.

Standing beside my pile of sleeping bags, I scan the room. The markers are not in my face like a treasure box, but there must be something. I search the room for a clue. My mind sees the horde returning. They will give up on Alice and Hugo because Alice and Hugo are smart, and it's hard to find people at night in a forest. But then Alice and Hugo are decoys and will put themselves out there until I find the diary. But the offensive linemen can't protect the Quarterback forever if there is no one to throw to.

"Step up!" Did I say that, or was that Hugo in my ear again?

It's not hidden. Because she would never guess that I'd be here looking for it. No. It is hidden. Because she's not her, and she would not just leave it lying around. Maybe it's on her. No. Because she doesn't want to be found with it on her, and she doesn't need it.

I scanned the room again. Up the fireplace? In the oven? I shook my head. The search could take days not minutes.

I might be hyperventilating. I can hear my heart in my ears. One, two, three...still beating, no cardiac arrest. Here is where I need to, according to Hugo, stop thinking so much, trust myself and my team, and give it my best effort.

OK, the play is: I read the room, look for holes, or weak spots, weak players.

She must have taken it with her. She could ditch it if she had to. Plenty of much better places to toss it in the forest where nobody would find it and the rain and snow would ruin the pages and the words on them. But she'd lose control of it then. If she went back, she might not find it.

So, if the diary IS here, all I've been doing is standing and waffling like a dog between two bones while Hugo, Alice and Andrew are taking the heat, probably tackled with bloody noses and split lips, all to find my stupid diary.

I open every cupboard in the kitchen, every drawer. I am an insane version of myself, whirling, hacking, jabbing. Nothing. I stop and stand in the middle of the room. I do a slow turn, peering into lightless corners. I see flush toilets beyond cracked open doors. There are toilets here. The water is turned off. Peter-Andrew said it belongs in a toilet. I check the backs of toilets of two bathrooms.

I try a third door. "It's locked," I say thinking out loud. "Why would this be locked and from the inside? Someone is there, hiding, because I've been making a lot of racket. Protecting themselves, something—hang on, this lock is the kind of lock that has a key. It locks from the inside and the outside. This is the adult's bathroom."

Gran never puts a key to anything in the same place twice. It's her way of confusing robbers and me. Sometimes she locks up and goes forgetting that I am not at home and without keys. She's locked Andrew and me out on bowling night, and senior center bingo night. Also, our bathroom lock is dicey and locks itself frequently. Andrew bought me a set of lock picks, with which I'm pretty handy, but I don't have my tools. I go back into the kitchen to look for substitutes. Because the boy scouts have badges of all types, eureka, I find a set. I love the boy scouts.

It's unlocked, but I hesitate in opening the door. There are five stages of human brain development, according to our eighth-grade biology teacher. "The prefrontal cortex, class, is the last to develop. That means that you all have poor control of impulses and poor decision making. That includes irrational and irritable behavior," she said as she took away the pencils Tom was drumming with.

In my mind, I see a person, sitting on the toilet with a gun trained on the door. My mouth dries, and I feel an electric jolt of panic bullseye my nervous system.

Pfffttt, as the commercial goes, just do it.

I stand aside and push so hard the door slams against the wall behind it. No shot, no yelling. I step in, my paint gun up. I check behind the door. I am so relieved that I nearly have to use the toilet.

All the bathrooms have been one-toilet jobbies, no stalls. At each stop, at each john, my great idea is becoming not such a great idea. Locked door…I'm praying, because this is my last-chance toilet. If this isn't it, I have to start over. I heavy-lift the lid off the back of the toilet, and I feel my body levitate. I see the diary. As I reach for, it my heart does a fish-out-of-water flip. Happiness is never lasting. I hear returning voices outside.

I don't want to be trapped here. I really, really don't. There are three exits out of the place, one third chance to get it right. I dash out the wrong one, but at least I take them by surprise. I'm like some dumb frightened animal that's caught and careens into the woods. I dash out the door for my life.

Also, I take the door that leads in the opposite direction to the way I want to go. Also, also, I'm not sure if these zombies are returning from chasing Hugo and Alice, or whether they are returning after finishing their work doing my diary page fifteen.

Like a football, I've got the diary securely tucked under my good arm. Out with my bad arm like a battering ram. If I actually hit anybody with it, I will probably fly through the air in pain. So really, it's actually good that I'm not flattening anybody, and I am getting through. Hugo's football Bible is correct about surprise. No real gain, though. They are turning to run after me.

I see a row of some six cabins. I run and grab the doorknob on the first one. Locked…locked…locked…locked…locked. All flipping locked! There are just screens on the windows anyway. I cut between cabins and see a very large corrugated building with no windows. No doubt locked.

Don't even try.

I rarely listen to myself, and I head to it anyway, because it is big and secure looking. There is also a house just beyond it. I don't make it to any of them. Something hits my back; my feet lose rhythm. I fall on my bandaged arm. I'm not just breathing dirt, I have it in my mouth, eyes and nostrils, and down my shirt. I am on my last life.

There is no fumble. Technically the ball is dead but this isn't a game and there are no rules.

I roll onto my back and shoot orange with an Andrew-enhanced machine-gun-quality paint gun. I'm firing blindly. As with any undead, they take the hits. Arms up to protect their faces, and heads angled down, but they keep coming, one step at a time through the paint. They are waiting for the click of an empty magazine. I am waiting for the click too. I have more balls, but there is no reloading, and they are getting closer. I think of my stink bombs, smoke bombs. No time to light anything.

Rocks hit my face, my arm. The pain is making my eyes water and my nose run. I get to my feet and turn. There's a heavy-duty, wooden, worktable. I dive behind it, taking the table with me onto its side. From the table, the remains of last year's metal crafting fall around me, the silver and rusted-orange heads of metal and solder, double-headed battle axes, flanged maces, and just to be different, a few corseques—for their medieval weaponry badges no doubt. Just for giggles, there are even poleaxes and one mounted on an actual pole. It's double edged with a pike out the top. Boy Scouts are scary and once again, I so want to be one.

I pick up an axe head. Not sharp. I toss them like big throwing stars. I hope that just having an axe coming at them will make my fellow classmates dive, belly to the ground. The rocks stop. Behind the table, I light three stink bombs and two smoke-pepper bombs and send them out as well. When a smell like skunk reaches me, and I hear coughing, I raise up like a submarine telescope. I and the pole axe try to disappear into the woods.

One good thing, I've left the flood-lit area. Well, that would be good if I still had my goggles. As I run, tripping over brush, trying to make out trees before I whole-body smack them, I think that people I've gone to school with for thirteen years have been pelting me with rocks. That could cause Takotsubo syndrome—chest pain, shortness of breath from a broken heart, the left ventricle of the heart ballooning. There is permanent damage. *I should sue.*

I find a narrow path which is good because I'm short and getting over dead, fallen trees with their giant dagger-like limbs is slowing me down. I hear a disturbance in the brush. Maybe it's Alice or Hugo. The thought cheers me. I think of hiding and waiting. If it's not, then I've given up my lead. But I have to breathe. I veer off the path and squat behind a three-foot diameter log.

I inhale and inhale and inhale and inhale and listen. My chest or side or something hurts, and my arm is bleeding again. I collapse deep into the cupped indentation at the base of a tree. My mouth is dry. I'm glad Alice made us wear heavy clothing, or the rocks and the limbs that are weapons on the fallen trees would have cut me. I have the pole axe on the ground beside me. I shift it to lay upright against the log.

Though I haven't heard more than birdsong since I stopped, I should keep going. Maybe I've lost them. It's a big forest, but that's not a Murphy's Law sort of attitude. I peer out and see no one and no movement. I stand, take a step, and turn my ankle. I fall back against the tree. I hear a laugh as five zombies step out of hiding.

One of them, Jamie Handley, who body slams people during capture the flag in gym class, dashes towards me. I point the pike head of the pole axe at her. It stops her, but she is only a decoy while the rest of her team surrounds me. This is not what they meant for this experiment, the adult powers that be. But seriously, how could they have, in any universe, assumed otherwise.

I am not a lot of things, not a tennis player or a golfer or anything that requires the self-confidence to stand alone and hit a ball while everyone is watching. I can't flip or handstand, but after all the swimming, I can run. I have short legs and now they are moving like the legs of a two-year-old between rushed adults. If my ankle is sprained, it's just going to have to wait awhile.

The one thing about the Boy Scout camp that's different from the girl scouts is that the girls sleep in cabins. Except for the few locked cabins for the adults, the rest of the place is bare down to the pine trees and brush. The boys have to tent it. Push comes to shove, I would lock myself into one of the many latrines, but there are no doors. Boys! And then I see a climbing wall.

Please don't be locked. Please don't be locked.

They are so close that I'm anticipating the smell of their pizza breath.

It is, with my luck of the damned, locked with a Master Lock Bluetooth padlock…fancy-schmancy. I hit the lock with the head of the pole axe using all the force I have in me. Three desperate, panic-driven hits. The lock holds. I throw my body at the door until the screws in the hardware that the lock is attached to give. Ya Baby! My fierce self! I duck inside, and then I close the door and lean hard against it. When my body stops shaking, I brace the pole axe against the door to keep out their pepperoni-breaths. It won't hold for long, but then they will have to fight me one at a time through a hole in the floor at the top of the stairs. I call for Hugo and Alice on my radio. I hear nothing but the pounding of bodies against the door and the screech of taunting voices. I reach the top platform and slide down the wall to sit. I can't hold back tears. I can't press pause. I can't get away.

Chapter Nineteen

Megan Cottrell, Mary Grey, Tina Maish, Carol Hart, people who don't choke in social situations, are now all injected, their minds a pulsating mess of thoughts. My long-time classmates jeer at me from the ground.

Carol is a girl with muscles. She plays sports, mostly baseball. Her dad coaches. She has a pretty face and blonde hair. One time, we were stacking chairs after a class, and she had a chair in her hands, and she was all—I can't get it to the top of that stack—to Seth who took it from her, all gallant-like. Then she was all thanks, and she was tossing her blonde hair. That girl could slug a heavy weight softball out of the park and into the park across town. Seth is half her size. It's acting.

I can't act. Gran says that I'm honest to a fault.

My life is playing out in my mind, every mistake, every embarrassment. I need to get control. When you're out-played, punt, before you hyperventilate, before the horde swarms up the side of the rock-climbing wall…like spiders or red ants, or volcanic lava, scratch the lava. It goes downhill.

Options: an eagle swooping down and carrying me off, Hugo arrives and charms them all, a zombie charmer, Alice has a back-up army from that closet of hers.

The people I have known all my life are still yelling up at me, calling me names.

Stop the insanity!

Pressing the communicators' talk button as if it is a tree and I am a woodpecker, I call out to my teammates. I'm expecting to hear, not Peter-Andrew, or Hugo, or Alice, but a high-pitched, harsh voice… we have your little dog. I'm not sure it's good or bad that I get only silence back, but I am seriously getting light-headed from panting.

I backhand the snot running from my nose. I raise my hip because something is gouging into it. I remember the carbon saber. I'd forgotten about it. Ok, realistic options. I can wait for them to climb and then go out the door. Problem, the people coming up the stairs. Voices are rising, getting closer. The thump of feet and hands rattle the structure around me. I stare at the top of the wall. I expect the first fingers to grab the lip at any time.

And then I hear the door below crash open. So much for the pole axe. I jump to my feet. Like a caged animal, I circle my space. I see that I was leaning against a half door. A new door is good. On the other side of it is a small platform and a thick wire that I can only now see because the moon is high. Hallelujah, it is a blessed zip-line, but again luck of the damned, no harness-sled.

There are feet on the stairs. Carol's head tops the hole in the floor. As she threads her arms through, I reach into my pocket for the rest of my smoke bombs. I pile them together with a handful of my loose wooden matches like a Boy Scout setting a fire. As she is about to get a leg up, I lunge at the top half of her torso with my saber. She ducks and falls down a few stairs. See, it does look real. Her chin took a bashing, and she is swearing at me. She realizes she is a bleeding, sitting duck if she puts her head through the hole again. Still, she can bench press seventy pounds, and all she needs is one mistake on my part to hoist her body through. I picture my body being thrown over the side of the climbing wall. That would be an exit of sorts.

I have to keep her on the stairs. I see her face in the hole. Her smile is evilly triumphant as we both see fingers on the lip of the platform wall. As I deal with the climbers, she will be up and out. Also, she has my escape blocked. The only way out is flight. I drop one lit match into the center of my pile, and I open the small door and step out onto the small zip line platform.

Behind me Carol is rising and saying things like, "You'll get yours," and, "Witch," and stuff. I have no harness. Once I jettison myself down the line, I don't know how I will stop. I don't know where the line goes. Should I take off my shirt? What else do I have? Shoes, shoes laces. I feel the carbon saber in my hand. I don't know if the saber will take my weight, or just snap in half sending me three stories to the ground, but it's all I have. It may burn up as I slide. Carol must be in the building by now. I place the sword on the wire and grasp its blade. I toss myself into the air.

I wait for the snap, but the saber holds. It's good to be a compact and lightweight person. Also, now I'm glad the weapon has no edge. My blood drips down my arm and blows into my eyes. I blink to clear them. I have to be able to see the end. My legs have to take the force of a fall. Breakage, I lose. One leg already has a sprained ankle.

The carbon in the sword is sparking. My hand is being burned. The wound on my arm is totally reopened. I see the end box. It's not far, maybe not far enough. There is a breaking mechanism on the line, but I am not riding down on a sled. Just before impact, I let go and drop about ten feet. My knees give. I roll, and I fall on my bad arm AGAIN. Still, I have my legs.

I gain my feet only to fall again, on both arms, at least, this time. I see a trail, and I struggle to stand and then to run. Branches whip me. I am jumping over logs like a drunk elephant rather than a graceful gazelle. I have the book tucked into my shirt and under my protective, undamaged arm. I have to make the goal. I have to get to Andrew and the boat. I don't know where Hugo and Alice are, but I have to get the boat away to a safer place.

I nearly kiss the main road as I reach it. I pound down the dirt road to the beach. Then I remember Peter-Andrew. "SET OFF THE DIVERSIONS," I yell into my walkie-talkie. "SET OFF THE DIVERSIONS!" And then I remember that I haven't heard from him all night. I think about setting off all the traps, but what I really want is to get to the boat and paddle to the island. I'm running like the wind to my touchdown.

All the time, I'm running, all the time that my back is to the zombies, I anticipate the sound of gunshots. My back anticipates a blow. My mind cringes in its imagination of blood and pain and holes in my heart. I run so fast that I may be hovering over the ground, like I'm at the speed of light. That's good, because if I'm caught, I'm dead. There is enough crazy out there.

I'm tiring. My feet are heavy. If I trip once, I'll never recover. I can't stop to light the diversions. There are back-up matches, but I can't stop, and then one explodes behind me. I jump out of my skin. My feet are out of sync, and I hit the ground.

I'M SHOT! I'M SHOT!

I wait for pain and death, but nothing happens. I push up to my elbows. As I spit out a tooth, I remember my signal to Peter-Andrew. Oh thank God!!!! The booming is music to my ears. The Fourth of July has begun behind me. Smoke and dirt and stink color the air. I rise from the dead and run. As I slip under the Waterfront sign, I jump the fireworks there that have begun to sizzle. I have to get to the beach before the tennis balls smack me. My lungs are burning, but the boats are near, and Peter-Andrew is still in one. I round the last corner. He's never looked so dear to me. I race down the dock.

"Do you know where Hugo and Alice are?"

"Geez, Elmur, what happened to you?"

"Have you heard from them?"

"Nobody. I called. Were you all out of range?"

"Oh man, we gotta go. We have got to go! They have the hidden boats. We'll wait for them on the island." My arm is numb, and even though the ropes are loose, I'm struggling with the tie-knots.

"We're leaving them?"

"Everyone is literally right behind me. And I mean literally."

As if on cue in a bad movie, the other team flies out of all corners of the forest behind the beach. I am about to push out the nose of the kayak, and the thump, thump, of the tennis balls being ejected from their cannons, has become a base rhythm to the hallelujah chorus in my head. We are going to make it. Praise Allah, we are going to make it.

We've all gotten this far without anything really deadly, so when a shot sounds, I am startled.

The fireworks have finished. The fireworks and the bombs sound like gunfire, like we have been firing.

And then Peter-Andrew yells out.

Shitnanigans, Andrew's shot.

My head snaps laterally, my eyes on Andrew. He is standing. I am so relieved that it takes me a hyper-second to process that, hang on, he is STANDING. Not only standing, but about to try and walk on water. I spin around to follow his line of sight. Someone is on the ground, Peter Farber, the real one. Peter-Andrew has seen himself, his own body, shot; seen his own body on a free fall to the ground; seen his own body bleeding; seen his own body beginning to die.

Zombies are still running onto the beach from the trees. So many more. Reinforcements. They are yelling, and brandishing weapons, but sometimes things just become clear to me. Maybe my brain is working on problems the whole time, or maybe that one last piece my thoughts are searching for falls into place. Mostly, it's too late, but today, right now, it's like the fog in my brain parts and lets some light in…and I get it. I pound down the dock like the front-line tackle that Hugo has been desperately trying to get me to be, the front-line tackle that my mother so disliked.

"SHUT IT DOWN! ANYBODY SHOOTS ANYBODY ELSE, IT WON'T BE CONSIDERED AN ACCIDENT," I scream as I hit the beach, my stride unwavering. "IT WILL BE MURDER." I am screeching so loud that I can hear myself over the pounding in my ears. Thanks be to God for my loud, projecting, genetic voice. My eyes must be all wild and terrible. Along with my hair streaming out around my head in dirty, ropey strands, like I put my finger in an electrical socket, that vision of me as blood-in-the-eye crazy, berserker seems to be keeping the horde back for the moment.

"WHOEVER HAS A PHONE, CALL AN AMBULANCE!" I dive to Peter's side, and as a good hospital volunteer, I push on his pectoral muscle, so close to his heart. Pressure on the wound.

I am a sitting duck. I wait for the injected to become unstartled. I wait for a shot that might join my body to his. I am low over his body, protecting him, or me, or both. There is so much blood coming out of him. There is just so much blood.

"WHO'S CALLING THAT AMBULANCE?"

"I'M CALLING."

I don't know who. I don't care.

"Why are you here? Why are you walking?" I ask the real Peter Farber so quietly it's kind of to myself and kind of to Peter.

Peter-Andrew is sobbing beside me. The real Peter is looking at me, his eyes pleading. They are both, the real and the fake Peter, saying to me not to let him die. "Someone has called an ambulance. They are going to be here. The ambulance is coming. You're going to be fine," I say as I press harder. I'm red. The ground is red. When I hear sirens, I feel the most joy and the most dread that I've ever felt in my life.

The beach is not populated by the time the cops arrive. That group, drunk or sober, addled or injected, knows how to hotfoot it from a police raid. The cops find me again, this time bent over a kid with a gunshot wound. The day is getting better and better.

I have to explain to the cops and the emergency crew why Peter-Andrew has to accompany himself to the hospital, and why I have to go with them in ambulance and not in the squad car. I am covered in blood. I think I'm having my own break-down because I scream at them when they try to pull me away. I wish I had been given the shot so that all this looks less like my fault. Authorities are always so righteous. I have to point out my arm, and that I need treatment before they let me get into the ambulance.

Telling them about the campout, the guns, and the injected kids in the forest can wait, can wait forever. I won't tell them to find Hugo and Alice, either. I don't want them to be a part of the end game. I pray so hard that that is a good decision. Then it occurs to me to say that they really, really have to look for anymore hurt people because the injected had access to guns and other weapons, and they went crazy. All the truth.

I stand and wait next to the ambulance as they load Peter Farber. I see the cops bring in teens that they are finding. Many are soaking wet. The backpack water guns worked. Go Hugo and Alice.

~

Peter-Andrew and I are left together as Peter Farber is gurney-raced down the corridor. Peter-Andrew is not allowed to follow. I take him with me to get the gash on my arm cleaned and stitched, again.

We sit close in the emergency waiting area. We are Victorian waifs, dirty, smelly, roughed up, and bloody in a sterile world. Well, I am dirty, Peter-Andrew is just wet and bloody. One mother is trying to not to stare at me, and at the filthy, stringy, bloody bandage that is almost not wrapping my arm. We are quiet for a while. It has been a long night. What do you say anyway to someone who has just seen himself get shot?

I'm called to a room. I have Peter-Andrew by a firm grip, and I won't let him go any more than I'd let my arm be cut off, which, looking at it, might be a possibility. The police follow Peter-Andrew and me but are kept out of the room.

The nurse leaves and as I change into a gown, I reach into my shirt and pull out the diary. I'm sitting on the white paper on the examining table, and I place it on my lap.

"You got it." There is a small injection of joy and awe in Peter-Andrew's voice

"Yeah."

"A lot of anger in there."

"Yeah."

We both study it like it has taken on a life of its own and might bite us. It is more than my diary. It's the book that launched a thousand ships and may have killed one kid.

"What do I do with it?"

He takes the book. I think he might open it and read some, but he doesn't. Maybe he doesn't want to remember me by my hateful words. He takes it to the hospital room sink, and he places it in. He turns on the water, full blast.

I hop down to watch the ink run down the drain. The words disappear like they never were. Peter-Andrew tears out pages and mixes them with more water creating a grey mass, and then he wrings out portions. He tears some the wordless white paper from the exam table and wraps it around the pulp. And then he walks out the door to toss it far, far away, preferably into another galaxy.

~

Gran arrives in the timeout area in the hospital like a spitting, yelling, football coach whose prime player has been damaged by excessive force and has been hit and is lying on the ground, out cold. The police want to take me away for questioning, but Gran taught all of them in kindergarten, and she says in a very insistent, loud voice that echoes down the hallway and into the street that I'd been through enough and the rest of it could wait.

She takes us to intensive care. With only two allowed at the bedside, Gran goes to visit some sick friends, two birds with one stone, and leaves Andrew's mom to sit outside the ICU.

I hold Peter-Andrew's hand, and we watch the heart monitor that is connected to Peter Farber.

"You're not dead," I say towards the hospital bed.

The only sounds are mechanical, the air smells like ammonia.

"Been over twenty-four hours. The injection is getting a little weaker," Peter-Andrew says. "I don't think it's going to last three weeks."

I squeeze his hand. "Really? That's great. Ahhhh. Peter, you not going to cease to exist. You are not going to die."

"Who do you think I was…he was injected with?" Peter-Andrew asks me; then he addresses the boy on the bed who is hooked up to all sorts of machines. "You stupid idiot, you let yourself walk."

"Don't yell at yourself. I mean, you know. It was a hard thing."

My arm is clean and wrapped in tons and tons of fresh, white wrapping. I'm beginning to like the color white. Grey is too messy. It is erased problems, missteps, and thoughtlessness.

"Maybe Peter got Stew "pid" Nelson," I say.

We both snicker, but not in a joyful way, and the times settle back on us like a deadly fog. "I guess I shouldn't have called Stewart Nelson that." I realize that old habits are going to die hard. We are quiet again and watch the patient continue to breathe.

"It's weird watching yourself die." Peter-Andrew, both of them, seem already in mourning. The injected Peter half of Peter-Andrew for himself, and the Andrew half of Peter-Andrew for a personality he's come to like.

"You're...Peter Farber is not dying. He is right there breathing." I said it strong, but inside I could feel my liquids rushing up to fall from my eyes. Distraction time. "Hey how does it feel to walk again? Finally."

"Do you think his legs are ruined forever?"

Oh for the love of Pete, think Laura.

"Nah, might just take a little longer. Every body part will be in the pink at the same time."

The vitals-monitoring machines are loud with at least eight patients in the ICU. Life is tenuous.

"Where did you stash the diary?"

"In every toilet I could find."

"That's where you suggested I put it before the whole thing started. That's where she hid it. It's a good place."

"I'm glad you didn't get a leather-bound edition or something."

"Couldn't afford it. It wasn't a leather-bound sort of book anyway."

"Write and flush. No paper trails."

We laugh. We have to; it's all been so out-of-body. Out the window the sky is once again turning blue, like nothing has happened.

"Where are Hugo and Alice do you think?" he asks.

"I keep thinking about them too. I didn't want to say anything to anybody in case they got away. I didn't want to get them into it. I hope that the people chasing them were not totally crazy. I didn't hear any guns, but the one."

I choke on the words that I want to eat. My heart breaks looking at the Peter in Peter-Andrew looking at himself.

"Anything could have happened to them," he says.

"I know," I say and the catch in my voice matches his.

Chapter Twenty

The smell of pine in the air is stronger. The sap has defrosted. The lake is warming under higher temperatures, and rain has been filling the basin. The bluebells of spring have come and gone. The thimbleberry and poppy are in bloom. The young adult restrictions have lifted. The injections have officially worn off. Tomorrow is the first day back to school since the I-ness Experiment-enforced three weeks' break. We will all be together for last three weeks before the end of school year.

Young adults have been restricted to their homes until the plague lifted. I haven't seen Andrew for three weeks. Probably would have happened anyway, as Gran grounded me. That trust she had; she says is gone. I should have come to her. I have seen the inside of the police station, but not for long. Gran called in her brother who threatened to sue the police for harassment of a minor. They have always had a reputation for being turdis maximus's anyway. She let them know that I figured it all out and stopped the vandalism. She also went after the school for being basically stupid. The jet ski was unharmed and just needed draining, which I did. Jet skis expect to be overturned. Mrs. Keller lived, and I bought her some new sequins. I have to pay back the deduction on the hospital bill. I'm out on time served.

So is Andrew, who got off scot-free as one of the injected. We are in his back yard looking at his tent. First time I've seen it again. First time Peter-Andrew has been completely back to normal.

"So sorry, again."

"Hey, you had my back, as promised."

"Of course. So, the electrics do work?"

"Oh yeah, it just doesn't like to fold anymore, so not too portable."

We both gaze on its colored splendor in a moment of silence.

"I don't mind it. New layer of protection"

"It seems to have a candy-coated shell."

He bursts out laughing. "What a ride."

"Ya," I say and laugh too.

We go inside the tent and fire up the Easy-Bake Oven. "What was it like?"

"It wasn't like I had his memories or anything, more like I just knew what he was thinking how he understood things. People would talk to him, and he'd answer, and I think that I wouldn't have said that."

"You let him, you know, take over."

"He seemed to care more about the answer. He wanted to talk. He liked to talk. I could feel that it mattered, how much he got out of it, the talking."

"And you got to sit back and let him do the work."

"Yeah. In a way, I kind of miss him. It was like watching a good flick. It worked you know. I got to see life from someone else's perspective. I hear on the news about deaths of injected kids in other countries. One jumped out of a building."

We are both quiet like we feel how serious it all had been. The weight of it. Dodging bullets.

"Knock, knock." We hear it from outside in Alice's voice. Andrew and I are having our first ever easy-bake party. "We brought the sparkling water."

The tent is really crowded, especially with Hugo, so we move out and into the sunshine.

"School tomorrow," Alice says.

She is looking at me with worry all over her face. I know why, I will meet Stella. She's in two of my classes. Actually, there are lots of people who have to see lots of people for the first time since the I-ness injections.

As with the other two of my new three amigos, Alice and I have been calling each other every day, and she told me that after she ran out of water and ammo, she ran. Like me, like hell hounds chased her. She didn't know which direction she ran except that she wasn't going to go towards the beach or Hugo. She was just trying not to trip, and then her feet sank into water.

"I was in the marsh, and all I could think of was *snakes*," she said. But she kept going into the freezing water, through the reeds and cattails, because she was sure that the hellhounds wouldn't follow. "They didn't. What they did do was guard the edge of the marsh so I couldn't get out. I was so cold. The chain mail was so cold, but I had to stay low.

I was afraid to get up or move. I didn't want the reeds to rustle. They were wet and paint balled. I got them good," she said with pride. "They were also angry and yelling terrible things. They said that I'd better dry off or my brace would get rusty. Like I hadn't heard that before. Be original, twits.

"My feet and hands went numb, and then I got kind of sleepy. I knew I had to get out of there. I didn't get back to you. I'm sorry. I wanted to, but when I found the bank of the marsh, I wasn't sure where I was. I walked and tried not to meet anybody. I got a little scared. I wasn't sure if I was walking away from the lake.

I walked so long in that bleeping forest, miles and miles. Finally, I found a path and stayed on it. My feet felt like raw meat. I kept walking. I stumbled onto a dirt road. *Yay*, I thought, *I'm saved.* I sat right in the middle of the road to rest. I was so quiet that I saw a bear cross the road in front of me, not too close, but…and I started crying. Nobody came. I got up again and walked until I got a signal on my phone. I called home. They were so upset. I was out of my brace for hours, da…da…da…. They didn't know I was gone. They didn't check because they didn't want to disturb all of us."

She also got grounded. She was delighted.

Hugo had his hands full with Stephanie. In their wisdom, the deciders—the principal and some teachers—had put direct opposites together. Me and Enid. Andrew and Peter, Stephanie, and Maddie. Stephanie is a girl who has been told from the age of five that she is special…if there is cake, take the biggest piece. She understands life at face value, not looking too deeply. She believes in whatever she is told. She believes it with strength and vigor.

Maddie is captain of the debaters. She can pull apart the statement, I am precious today. Since that statement is Stephanie's whole world, the girl was trying, in front of Hugo, to rip her own head off. She was like a person with brain damage who wears a helmet. She hit her head against trees. She yelled and wept and scratched and shook. She was not going fold to Maddie's point of view.

Maybe Stephanie recognized Hugo's soft touch, someone she could use, because she was like a leech on his skin. It was like she had a hundred tentacles for arms and legs and big pink suckers. At first, he had tried to keep going, misdirect, break-away from her cover. When she finally went totally insane, he had to do what he does, help her, and then he heard the gunshot.

He was on the second wave of ambulances. I heard Stephanie-Maddie arrive in the emergency room. She was screaming. Narcissists can be very fragile inside. I think she got a good dose of Valium or something. Hugo stayed with her until her parents got there.

We are drinking sparkling water out of champagne glasses and eating chocolate cake slathered with store-bought icing. Alice's chair is right next to Hugo's, and she is leaning against him brace and all. His arm encircles the metal. *Alice and Hugo*, I think, *perfectamento*. Best thing to come out of all this.

Alice stands and brushes the crumbs off her jeans. "Let's go see Peter. Take him a cake."

Peter Farber got out of ICU after the end of the first week. At the end of the second week his aunt paid me a visit. In her arms was a big box of chocolate and a dozen roses. "These are from Peter," she said at the door. "He told me to get them for you, and to bring them over, and to say that he has a second controller in the hospital. He won't be out for another two weeks. He's back to normal early. All the drugs and stress and hormones from the accident killed off the foreign cells. He feels foolish."

She's really young, like in her thirties. She told me that Peter's parents were killed when he was thirteen in a car accident. She was the baby of the family, ten years younger than Peter's father, but she took in Peter anyway.

"No one else," she said to me. "I won't lie, it has been difficult for both of us. He's told me about you from time to time. How you slugged some kid in the stomach for making fun of someone. He really admired you for that. And other stories about how funny you are."

You could have blown me over with a puff of air.

"Ya," I say to Alice. "I told him I'd for sure be there today. He's out in seven days, but still back in his wheelchair."

"You've had lots of practice with that," Alice says.

We all laugh.

~

Three weeks ago, we all walked into the school for the first day of Stepping Away from I-ness. Today, the first day back since, we all are walking into the first day of stepping back into I-ness.

Midday, in the cafeteria, I wait for Hugo and Alice and Andrew. I haven't seen Stella yet; she has second lunch and my classes with her are in the afternoon.

I try to open my milk. I always get the stuck-tight cartons with too much glue. I am tearing the top of the thing apart. It looks like mice have ravaged it. The lunchroom is full-on noisy. People are sharing who they think they hosted, if they didn't already have someone to clue them in. Andrew Frankenstein Holtus actually enjoyed the whole experiment. The only reason he knew who he was, was because I was there the whole time, as promised, and I could tell him. I watch Enid walk in. For a second, I wonder again if I'd missed something.

The injected act like they're now special, survivors with war wounds. They have a story to tell. Anne Hurley swears that her eyesight has improved. Janie Wilson says that she can play the piano a little. John, the body builder and football star, Fitzgerald gained twenty pounds from eating the whole time he hosted.

So then did the addition of me into Stella's blood stream create a kind of a super villain? I feel cool about that for some weird reason.

I bite into my peanut butter and jelly sandwich. The flavor of it is so familiar to me that I don't really taste it. I've been mostly eating peanut butter and jelly sandwiches at lunch for my lifetime at school.

Bernie Wilson gets up to move to another table. I sip from my semi-crushed milk carton. My thoughts are struck with the idea that that's who he is, Bernie, a room worker. He couldn't sit at one table if he tried. Same with Joan Palmer who likes black clothes, and Angie Robinson who closes her eyes when she drinks anything. Weird science, the science of genetics.

The experiment was a mix. Some of us were hit hard and some hardly hit, and some didn't have to deal with the head-case of having a two-voice mind. *Shenanigans*, the shenanigans of life.

It's like in war. When bombers hit a city night after night, some people die, some people live, some lose property, some don't, some people are scared out of their geezers every single night, some become gainfully employed as looters. Everyone is affected, even if it's just because the city is rubble. Same here. Our bomb changed lives. We carried on. Though some people had shrapnel, and some stayed on the edges, no one will forget. It's hard to see it, sitting here in the cafeteria, but some of us will never be the same.

With my second bite, I glance behind me at the entrance to the cafeteria. I warm inside when Alice and Hugo come in. He has his arm around her, around her brace. She laughs at something he says. She has become a great brace girl. When she sees me, she breaks from him and rushes straight over. I love this girl. She is an on-time, you-can-count-on-me-when-I-promise type of person. I really, really like that about her. I tell people stuff like that a lot now, that I like them, especially Alice because of what she did in the marsh.

Andrew comes in. I am so glad I have my friend back. So awfully glad that when I see him, it's like he is so much more precious to me.

"You haven't seen *her* yet, have you?" Alice says.

"No."

"You ok? Maybe we should walk with you to your next class, I mean you know, sudden emotions are so tricky."

When the lunch bell rings. We all stand. Trash is disposed of.

"It's all good," I say and wonder if I believe it myself. The place is even noisier now with trays being emptied and stacked. There is some laughter, and it sounds good.

People are happy to talk about their experiences in their safe groups, but we all are uncomfortable in the totality of each other. I am uncomfortable, anxious. Stella, I can't avoid her much longer. It's going to happen, and it's going to happen soon. I know what Alice is talking about. My mental fortitude might just become a hot, over cooked bowl of oatmeal mush.

While I am a mess of bruises and cuts, she is not any of it. She is unscathed. Trespassing dropped because she was injected and out of her mind, couldn't prove the vandalism. Only me torn, damaged.

Andrew, one of the injected, was let go. Hugo and Alice, well Hugo was saving Stephanie, and Alice wasn't found.

Best thing to do, is to quit looking for Stella. Quit scanning the crowd. I am not a rabbit looking for hawks.

Hugo, Andrew, and Alice peel away from my side to their classes. I am alone and walking the last bit of hallway to my next class. Maybe I am a rabbit checking for holes to dash into should I see her. It has been a bad morning like that, and the day isn't over.

When it finally happens, when I see her, my heart lurches from my chest. There is a shot of adrenaline to my brain. She is coming forward and people are parting in her wake like she is a naval destroyer and they are pleasure cruisers. It's like a scene in slow-mo. I didn't think that seeing her would slam me like a gut-punch. My body goes into fight or flight response, hyperarousal, acute stress. I'm so awash in adrenalin and cortisol, and norepinephrine that if anyone shot me now, I wouldn't feel it.

Am I walking towards her? I don't even know. I can't feel my feet or arms or fingers. Thoughts race from all points of my brain, chunks of sentences, isolated words, hate. My mind is desperate in trying to claw together some coherent thought. All the while her face is getting closer, more focused. She is laughing, LAUGHING!

Anger boiling up from my gut, all the pain she caused. Peter in the hospital fighting for his life, the scar on my arm that I will always have to remind me. I watch her, follow her every movement. She sees me, but is acting like she hasn't. She moves straight for me like a torpedo with a homing device. She will not step aside.

I was not injected with her, but still I know her now, how she thinks, who she is, what she is capable of.

I'm so angry I actually hear something in my brain pop. I am stroking out. Not hypertension, it's actually like a plug has been pulled, and my hormones are draining. Adrenalin, cortisol, norepinephrine swirl around and empty down the now-open pipe. My hands relax, and my shoulders. The tension in my face eases. She has been vetted, and she has been found lacking. Absodefinitely lacking.

From her lacking, a new way of looking at myself cracks open.

She continues towards me, closer and closer. She will not alter course. She will make me stand aside. Her eyes lock onto mine. A one trick pony.

I have a choice. Will I finally stand up for myself and body-slam her to the ground for all she has done? I can be ready to dart my foot out, to catch her ankle, to watch her straight, black hair fly up as she falls, to hear the crack of her largish nose as it hits the tile first. I have some tissue in my pocket that I can drop to her side for the bloody nose she would have. Should I sock her in her solar plexus so hard my fist goes up her body and knocks out her teeth? Done it before.

We are zeroed onto each other. People are moving to give us space. My heart is thumping in my ears. She is smiling, anticipating another victory, another notch in her belt, another humiliation at my expense. I feel the will of her mind and body pulling at me, directing me. I want to see her on the ground so much. I want my victorious foot on her back and her nose bleeding.

Pfffttt, she is the worst, most horrible person…but all that encompassing bubble of hate has popped.

It has popped, cannot be continued. The hate can't find that hard place in me that usually sustains it. Something new is there…gratitude. Gratitude for my new friends, for chocolate and roses from Peter Farber, for my gran, for

Andrew and his tent being whole, for the whole mess being over. It was my hate and hers that made all this happen. I'm done with that.

In the moment that we reach each other, it becomes clear to me, that I don't need to take her down. I don't need think about her ever again. Someday, I might even be able to say to her, good one, thanks for the sign. She is walking towards me in direct line with my path. I just stop where I am and let her come to me. What happens next is her decision. It will stand for what she is, what she has learned. I am watching her like I have all the time in the world and waiting. I see confusion in her eyes. They dart from me to the thickening, observant crowd. She is close enough now that I can count the two pimples on her nose, too much pizza. Ten more steps to where I stand. I brace myself, a reflex. She gives my shoulder a hard nudge with hers, like she's saying this isn't over yet. I laugh because it so is. It so is. She hasn't learned anything.

Booyah, you are so bang-up, so worthy. I tell myself. Why not, because what a shot in the arm this all has been.

"You are the hero of your own story," Peter said to me during one of my visits.

I have earned my bracelet. Thanks Principal Kaiser.

I finish walking to class as if something happened.

Made in the USA
Las Vegas, NV
22 November 2021